Summer Job

—Montana Beach—
Book 2

David Neth

DN Publishing

Summer Job
Montana Beach, Book 2

Batavia, NY

www.DavidNethBooks.com

Publisher: DN Publishing
Cover Design: DN Publishing
Proofreading: Laura Keysor

ISBN: 978-1-945336-77-5
First edition

Subscribe to the author's newsletter for updates and exclusive content:
DavidNethBooks.com/Newsletter

Follow the author at:
www.facebook.com/DavidNethBooks
www.twitter.com/DavidNethBooks
www.instagram.com/dneth13

Also by David Neth

Fuse series
Origin
Omertà
Oblivion

Montana Beach series
Summer Stay

Small Town Christmas series
A Christmas Reunion

Under the Moon series
The Full Moon
The Harvest Moon
The Blood Moon
The Crescent Moon
The Blue Moon
The Art of Magic

Anthology
Collateral Damage:
A Superhero Anthology

Standalone
All I Ever Wanted
Limelight
Snow After Christmas

Chapter One:

Robyn

My alarm wakes me at six in the morning. It's the first day of work this season at the Montana Beach Pier amusement park. Or just the Pier, as everyone calls it. I don't have to be at work for another five hours, but I want to squeeze in some painting time before the day gets started.

With my eyes slits from the cruel bathroom light, I brush my teeth before hopping in the shower, readjusting to my familiar routine from last summer.

I wish I could say I'm excited about starting the season again. I mean, I guess I am, but that's more to see the families stroll through the gates again. The kids are always so excited and they usually don't know which ride to try first. And then, by the afternoon, they're so hyped up on sugar and their parents are so drained from the sun that it makes for hilarious entertainment, even though I'm technically working.

But the door won't open to guests for another week. In the meantime, my employees and I have to get everything up to snuff for opening day. Which means they'll be cleaning up the rides after the maintenance guys check to make sure they're running okay and I'll be stuck in the office doing paperwork and getting our marketing materials together.

I step out of the shower, wrap a towel around myself, and walk into the second bedroom I use as part walk-in closet, part art studio. I don't have too many clothes, but I do have more than the tiny closet in my bedroom would allow. Still, there's enough space for my art supplies too. And all the paintings that are waiting to be sold. The perks of living alone, I guess. Anyway, I'm going to miss spending all day to paint the landscapes from around town, but I'll squeeze in time to keep painting when I can.

As I pick out clothes to wear, I try to remember everything I have to do when I go in today. I made a couple trips to the Pier office last week to start getting some paperwork started. I also hired two new people: a cleaner and a concession person, bringing our total number of employees up to fifteen. Including me. Not a lot, but it works.

Actually, I have another interview today. If he seems sane enough, I think I'll make him a ride operator. Out of the two other new employees, one is barely old enough to work, meaning I don't feel comfortable putting him in charge of a ride for kids under ten, and the other doesn't seem to even *want* a job, so I stuck her as a cleaner.

It seems mean, but that position is the easiest to make up for if we lose someone midseason. The guy I'm interviewing today might even spend half his shifts cleaning. We don't have the budget to hire too many designated cleaners, so everyone has to chip in.

Once I'm showered and dressed, I return to the spare bedroom and really look at my work in progress. It's starting to come together. I squeeze out some paint, dab in a brush, and get to work.

Usually I like to paint in the midst of my inspiration. *Plein air*, as it's called in the art world. It helps me really get in touch with my surroundings, but since I don't have a lot of time now that I'm working, I have to make do with a photo hanging on the wall above the canvas.

I work for a couple hours, filling out the canvas with more colors, bringing to life the sunrise scene that fills me with so many happy memories. Before I know it, it's just after ten and I rush to clean up my paints in the bathroom sink that's stained with colors from previous paintings; a work in progress itself.

Once I'm all cleaned up, I grab my bag and my keys and walk down to Atlantic Street, where there's a tiny little coffee shop on the corner with First Street.

"You're here early," Nancy says from behind the counter. "Your usual?"

"Yes, please," I respond. "It's my first day back at the Pier."

"Is it that time of year already?" She fills a to-go cup with a dark roast blend.

"Sure is. Creeps up faster each year."

"And passes by just as quickly!" She chuckles, passing me my order. "Here you go, dear."

I take the cup from her and hand her my card. "Maybe next year we'll be able to expand the season a bit, but I still need to whip my employees into shape. I've got a few new ones this year."

"I'm sure you'll be able to, honey. I'll have to bring my granddaughters down if I have time this year."

"Oh yeah! That would be fun!" I take my card back and slip it in my wallet. Slinging my bag back on my shoulder, I head to the door. "Thanks, Nancy. Have a good day!"

"You too, dear!"

My assistant manager, Peggy, is already in the office when I get to work. She's never early, so I must be a few minutes late.

She has her feet up on the desk and is filing her nails while she snaps her gum.

"Sorry I'm late," I mutter. She probably doesn't care.

"Oh, you actually came back this year."

"I just knew it would make your day." I boot up the computer and take a sip of my coffee.

"I see you still haven't found a real job," she says.

"And neither have you," I say as polite as I can.

This is our relationship each summer. Verbally jabbing each other under the veil of a joke. I think she might want me to quit, but it's not like the owners would make her manager. They live up in North Beach and own several attractions up there. This tiny little pier all the way down in Montana Beach isn't on their radar too much, but they're still funding our operations, so that's good. I can imagine the attractions up north are making a lot more money than we are, though.

If they're forced to hire a new manager for the Pier, it might be easier for them to just close it. That's where it was heading before I started. I trimmed the budget, beefed up policies, and started advertising to the right audience. In the three years that I've had the position, the annual number of visitors has gone up by thirty percent.

Of course, in the process of turning this place around, I had to lay a few people off, argue with the remaining employees about my new policies, and took on the reputation of *bitch*. Collateral damage for saving a small town business.

The intercom beeps and I look up to the camera and see some of the workers down by the gate.

"Peggy, can you let them in? I'll meet you guys out in the break room in a few minutes for the meeting."

She sighs loudly, but drops her feet to the floor and steps out of the office. I take another gulp of my coffee, nearly burning my tongue. It's worth it. It would be a long summer without it.

I gather my notes and step into the next room where everyone's putting away their belongings before they begin the day. I do a quick headcount. Still waiting on a few people. Everyone's supposed to be working today because I didn't schedule a full day of hours. I also wanted to be able to have a meeting with everyone at once.

I do my best to smile and welcome everyone back, but most people don't seem to have much enthusiasm. It's still early. They're just tired. Yeah, that's it. A lot of people have coffee with them. I shouldn't have left mine on my desk.

Once the rest of the crew arrives, I clear my throat to get their attention, but they all still talk loudly to one another.

"Hey!" Peggy shouts. She's standing off in the corner, still filing her nails.

Slowly, the room quiets as everyone turns to face me.

"Thank you. Well, welcome back for another season, everyone! We have some new faces here, so for starters, everyone please welcome Michael." I motion to him in the corner. He's a relatively quiet guy. Judging by his baby face, I'd say he's right around eighteen years old. "He will be working concessions. Our other new employee is Julia." She's sitting on one of the benches next to Peggy. Her blonde hair is pulled away from her face in a French braid. "She'll be working with Anthony this year to keep the Pier looking nice."

Only a few people look in their direction. The rest seem bored.

"All right, we have a lot to do today, but I need to take a moment to discuss one thing in particular. Some of you came in after your eleven o'clock start time. Now, I know it's the first day of the season and you're probably trying to get back into the routine, but let's make an effort to be on time tomorrow, okay?"

Ugh, I hate doing that. I know it just feeds right into the image that I'm a bitch, but it's the first day and the same people are late again. Not much changes around here, apparently.

"All right, so today—"

Someone with dark scruffy hair raises his hand in the back. Max Sherman. He was among those who showed up late. He always is. Actually, he's the worst. I shouldn't have asked him back, but I was desperate for employees.

"Do you have a question?"

"Yeah, what does it matter if we're late or not?" he asks. "It's not like there's people lining up outside. I didn't see anybody out there, did you guys?"

The room laughs and some people even respond with things like, "Haven't seen anyone here in years," or "Surprised this place is even still open."

Even if they haven't seen the numbers, they must know there's been more guests each year. It's kind of hard to miss for such a small amusement park.

I wait until the room settles down again and then address Max directly. "We usually start working a week before the Pier opens to get it ready for opening day, but with your attendance record, I'm not surprised that you didn't know that."

The room erupts again, this time with comments like, "Ooo, she got you, man!" or "Damn, boss lady's got jokes!"

"Anyway," I continue loudly to silence them. "You've all received an email with a checklist of everything we need to get done before the park opens—"

"What email?" Max asks.

"The one that went out a couple weeks ago."

"Oh that? I must've thought that was junk." He laughs.

Man, I wish I had more coffee this morning. "Next time, be more careful, please. Basically, what I said in the email was that the owners are sending in maintenance people today to make sure the rides run fine after the winter. What we need to do is get everything else opened up. That means sweeping, waxing, pulling out picnic tables and benches from storage, stuff like that. It's going to take time, but working together we can get it done."

Max chuckles.

"Is there a problem?"

"No, I just thought I was watching an after-school special all of a sudden."

More laughs. I'm about to snap at them, but everyone's attention turns to the guy standing in the doorway. Maybe it's because he's new. Maybe it's because he's the only one not in the Pier's uniform of blue polo and khaki shorts. Or maybe it's because his smile could change anyone's attitude. But the room goes silent when he steps in.

"Hi, sorry. The gate was open and—I didn't mean to interrupt. I'm Jaden. I'm here for an interview."

"Good luck," someone mutters.

I shoot a glare in their direction and a few people recoil. This is definitely *not* the way I wanted to start the season off.

Softening my tone, I turn back to Jaden and nod in the opposite direction. "Why don't you take a seat in the office and I'll be with you in just a sec?"

He nods and walks past me to the open door. When he's out of sight, I turn back to my employees.

"Look, I don't want to have to be the mean boss, but you guys leave me no choice. Our customer attendance has been up in recent years, but we won't get more people in here if we don't each take a more active role in making sure they have a good time. That starts with *all of us* having a good time. Don't get in the mindset that this place is horrible. Yes, it's a job, but we can have fun with it. Our attitudes will reflect on the guests and keep them coming back. That means we'll all be here again next year and the year after that. Okay?"

To my surprise, I see a couple people shrug and nod. That's

probably the best I'll get from these guys for right now. I'll take it.

"Okay, then. Let's get to work. Peggy, can you assign jobs for everyone while I meet with Jaden?"

She takes the clipboard from me and leads everyone outside.

I take a deep breath in the silence that follows and return to the office. Jaden looks up and smiles when I enter.

"Sorry about that." I extend my hand to him. "I'm Robyn, nice to meet you."

"Jaden," he says.

I take a seat behind the desk. "Just give me a minute to get organized here." I search for his application. I know I printed it last week when I was in. "So tell me a little about yourself."

"Well, uh, I just graduated college, I'm staying in Montana Beach this summer, and I'm looking for a summer job."

I dig through a stack of papers in the corner. I told Peggy to file these, but I guess it didn't fit into her schedule.

"Uh-huh." I'm not really listening, too busy looking under papers and in drawers for his application.

"Yeah. I've done some retail in the past, but never anything like this," he says.

Finally, I spot it still sitting in the printer and snatch it. I skim it and ask, "So you're done with school, then?"

"Uh—yeah, I am."

It sounds familiar and I scrunch my nose. "You just told me that, didn't you?"

He smiles. "Yeah, but that's okay."

"Sorry about that. I've been so frazzled with the opening that I'm not all here just yet. Anyway, so now that you're done, what are you hoping to do full-time?"

He shrugs. "I don't know. I'm just looking for something for the summer right now and then hopefully find something fun in September."

"Something fun," I murmur as I scan his application again. There's a retail job at a tourist store listed and a work study job, which must be from when he was in college, but not much else. "What did you do at your retail job?"

"I was a cashier, so I was kind of the face of the customer service for the store. It's a small place, so there were really only two of us working at a time. If a customer needed help and my coworker was busy, I kind of acted like a personal shopper."

I nod. "Oh, nice. We need great customer service at the Pier. So I take it you're good with money?" Not that he'd actually be dealing with money much here, but it's better to ask more questions than not.

"Oh yeah. My drawer was always spot on."

"Excellent." I skim the brief description he has for his work study job. "It looks like you worked for a photographer in college."

"Yup. I was basically his assistant. Setting up shots in the studio, adjusting the lighting, I even developed a few photos myself in the dark room."

"How cool. That must've been fun."

"Yeah, it was."

I hate doing short interviews, but there isn't a lot more to ask. He's had customer service experience, which is huge with us in order to get customers to keep coming back. This position isn't exactly rocket science. I just want to know I'm not hiring a jerk like Max.

"Where are you from?" I ask, just to draw out the interview longer.

"North Beach, but I'm staying over on Cemetery Street this summer, so transportation won't be an issue."

"What made you want to come to Montana Beach?"

"It's quieter."

I chuckle. "That it is. Sometimes too quiet. But luckily, this place is the epicenter of activity in town each summer."

"That's good. I figured it's a nice change of pace here, too."

"A lot slower of a pace."

He smiles. "Just what I'm looking for."

I cluck my tongue as I search his application for another question. I've pretty much exhausted my questions. He seems like a hard worker and there aren't any other applications in the system to review. *This* is the reason I have the types of employees that I do.

"What's your availability?"

"Immediately," he says. "I could start right now if you really wanted."

My eyes snap up from the paper. "Could you?"

"Are you offering me the job?"

I flash him a smile. "I guess I am. You're hired."

Chapter Two:

Jaden

"I'm going to stick you with Max for today," Peggy tells me as we walk down the length of the pier. I've never been here before, but it seems like a cool place. Everything looks older than the amusement park in North Beach, but it's almost vintage now. The most notable thing here is the Ferris wheel, which sits at the end of the pier overtop of the water. I can only imagine how windy it can get up there.

"What do you want me to do?" I ask. Robyn said she had some paperwork to take care of in the office, so she asked Peggy to get me acquainted with everything.

"We're cleaning," she says. "It's not rocket science. The folks who have been here the longest are cleaning and waxing the rides. You can help Max sweep and mop the deck and pick up any trash you see laying around. Make sure you're thorough." She hooks her thumb back to the office building. "Boss Lady in there nitpicks everything."

I nod. "Sounds easy enough."

Summer Job

There's a kid with shaggy hair at the end of the pier sweeping the deck when we approach. Max, I assume.

"Hey, I'm giving you a shadow today," Peggy tells him. "Don't do anything stupid. Show him what needs to be done and have him help."

"For how long?" Max asks.

She shrugs. "All day, I guess."

He groans and she takes that as her cue to walk away, which leaves me standing there awkwardly when he resumes sweeping.

After a few seconds he points back down the pier. "There are some brooms in the storage room. It's the door on the right of the office."

I nod and go retrieve a broom. When I return, Max is leaning on his broom, looking out at the water. Not wanting to say anything stupid, I start sweeping where it looks dirtiest.

"So you're the new guy, huh?" he asks.

"Yup," I say, still sweeping. "I'm Jaden."

"Max." He turns around to look at me. "I didn't mean for it to sound like I didn't want you hanging around. She just always has an excuse to have eyes on me."

"Peggy?"

He shakes his head. "No, Robyn."

"Oh, she doesn't seem so bad," I say. "Kinda cute, actually. This summer could be fun with girls like her around."

"*Cute*? You think Robyn's *cute*?"

I drop my head down again. "Guess not."

"Look, whatever she's got going for her will be quickly overlooked once you get to know her. She can be a real bitch. Makes working here a living hell sometimes."

Seems nice enough to me. "I'll have to watch out for that."

He leans in closer and drops his voice. "The moment you do something wrong"—he snaps his fingers—"you're put on her shit list."

"I've had some bad bosses before. I'm sure I can handle it." So far, Robyn's not like any of them.

He starts sweeping again, pushing his pile over the edge of the pier. "What made you want to work here anyway?"

"Thought it could be fun," I say. "It's not quite as hectic as North Beach down here."

"Is that where you're from?"

I nod. "Yeah. It's basically tourist city. Figured I could spend a summer in a quieter place like this."

"Montana Beach is basically dead," Max says.

"I don't know about that. It's tiny, that's for sure, but there seem to be quite a few people who live here."

"Have you noticed there's only one place to stay in town? Unless you want to rent a house, but that can get expensive. Still, there's enough of them."

"Yeah, I'm renting one of the houses, actually."

"You are?" He wipes the surprise from his face. "Rich parents?"

I shake my head. "No, just working here. It *is* expensive, but I'll be just able to squeeze it. Actually, the house has two bedrooms, so if I had a roommate, I could split the cost."

His eyes grow wide. "Really?"

I shrug and push the growing pile of dirt in front of me. I don't want to push it over the edge. I might be new here, but I know that that's just lazy. "Yeah. It's not a big house, but it's nice. Not too far from the beach, either."

"Well, nothing in this town is too far from the beach."

"True."

"I've been meaning to get out of my parents' house for a while now," he says. "I would love to have my own place. I'm jealous."

I know what he's looking for and even though I don't really know him, I should probably find a roommate sooner than later if I'm going to be able to use any of the money I make working here on things *other* than the bills. Max has got a job and it's only for the summer.

"You could stop by after work and check it out if you're interested in taking the extra room at my place. It's a nice house."

He smiles. "Awesome, I definitely will. You mind if I hitch a ride with you?"

I shake my head. "I don't have a car here, but it's only over on Cemetery Street. We can walk."

"Oh, well that kind of sucks, but I guess it's not too far. Thanks, man!" He holds out his hand and I clasp it and give him a quick pat on the back.

"Looks like you two are getting along pretty well," Robyn says as she comes around the towering Ferris wheel.

"I was just showing him everything we need to do to open." Max quickly resumes sweeping, moving faster to get away from Robyn.

"Do you mind if I steal him for a bit?" she asks him, pointing to me. "I want to give Jaden the grand tour."

Max scoffs. "Okay, see you in five minutes."

Robyn ignores him and leads me around the corner. "Well, obviously this is the Ferris wheel. It's the oldest attraction on Montana Beach Pier and the only one open to adults as well as kids. It has survived wind storms, hurricanes, and even a little bit of snow."

"No lightning?"

"Well, I'm sure it's been struck a few times," she admits. "But not since I've been here."

"How long's that been?"

"This is my third year as the manager. I was a ride op for several years before that, though."

"What's my position?"

Her eyebrows jump up in surprise. "Oh, I'm sorry! I never

told you. I'm going to train you to be a ride op too, so you'll be one of the people in charge of running the rides."

I look up nervously at the Ferris wheel. "Are you sure you can trust a newbie with that? What if I go too fast and kill someone?"

Robyn rolls her eyes. "Nobody's died here. But if you did, that would at least get us some publicity." She smiles to show she's joking.

I laugh. "That's so bad."

"I'm kidding, obviously. No, the controls are pretty easy. It's basically all automated now, just as long as you press the right buttons and wait until you get the all-clear signal from your coworkers. We'll have Bailey or Mackenzie or someone train you and you can shadow them until you get comfortable with it. You'll be fine."

"That shouldn't be so bad, then." I follow her over to the next ride, a long kiddie roller coaster. Each car is painted to look like ladybugs.

"This one is the most popular kiddie ride here, although it breaks down a lot of the time because it's so old. It's been here since the seventies, I think."

"Oh wow. Time for an upgrade." The metal fence surrounding the ride is rusted with a few rungs missing.

"I wish we could upgrade, but the owners haven't given us any extra money for repairs or replacements."

"Why not?"

She shrugs. "We're small fry compared to what they've got going on up in North Beach. You probably know what I'm talking about, right?"

I nod. "Yeah, there are a million different gimmicky entertainment venues. It's crazy up there."

"That it is."

Robyn takes me throughout the rest of the Pier and points

out the other rides. There's a kiddie Ferris wheel for those too afraid to go on the big one. They also have a carrousel, a few midway games, and a stage where they try to get people to come and entertain.

"It's been getting harder to get people to come do a show for the kids," she admits. "But I think I have it booked up for most of the summer. That'll buy us some time to book the rest of the season."

The stage butts up against the Pier's office. The curtain the workers are reinstalling looks worn and torn, the stage itself looks flimsy, and there's nowhere for anyone to sit.

"Looks like this could use an upgrade too," I note.

She nods. "And I'm sure we'll get more money to upgrade everything as soon as we start making more money. It's kind of a catch-22."

"I can see that."

"So you're catching on that we're doing the best we can with what we have to work with?"

I nod. "I get it."

Robyn looks down the pier toward the Ferris wheel. Max is still sweeping, although he's moved closer to the ladybug ride.

"Well, that's the tour," she says. "It isn't much, but it's our world for the summer."

I shrug. "It's very manageable."

She smiles. "You're sweet. She looks up at Max again and adds, "You better go back and help him. Maybe he'll pick up the pace."

"You got it, boss."

§ § §

"I DON'T KNOW why I thought this year would be any different," Max whines on the walk to my house after work. "Each year she gives me the same crappy jobs. Sweep the deck, mop the deck, clear the trash bins, scrape off the bird poop. It sucks! I don't know why she's singling me out."

"Aren't you one of the cleaners?"

"Well yeah, but it seems like she's always picking on *me*. Never Mackenzie. Never Carl. Always me."

"But you've been there longer than anyone else, right?" We stop at the corner of Third Street and Montana Boulevard and wait until it's clear to cross.

"I mean, I guess so. I don't know. Still seems to me like she's on a power trip this year."

I stare down at the cracked sidewalk as we get closer to Cemetery Street. "You *were* kind of giving her attitude this morning when I came in."

"Who's side are you on, man? Are you defending her?"

"No—I mean—I'm just saying, I can see where she's coming from. But look, today was my first day, so I don't know what I'm saying."

"Well, you don't know her like the rest of us," he says. "She can be nasty."

I doubt that, but I keep my mouth shut. Max and Peggy have both already made it clear that most people at the Pier don't like Robyn. If I want to keep the peace with them—especially if Max becomes my roommate—I need to tread carefully. Still, I think it's unfair the way they're completely writing off Robyn so early in the season. She seemed really nice to me.

And I'm standing by my cute comment.

My house sits right next to the old motel in town. There's a long wooden fence along the property line that's overgrown with weeds and vines, but at least it's better than staring at a cracked, forgotten parking lot. The house is a small bungalow with a wide front porch and a peaked roof. It's actually in very good condition for being a rental.

"Oh wow, this place *is* nice," Max says as we approach. "I thought when you said it was nice earlier that you meant there were no bugs, but this is a *house*."

I pull my keys out of my pocket with a grin. "Yeah, it's pretty sweet."

"How'd you get ahold of this?"

"It was in the paper."

"Fair enough."

I unlock the door and step into the open great room that serves as the living room, kitchen, and dining room all in one. Through the kitchen, there's a door that leads to a covered back porch. To the left is the hallway leading to the two bedrooms and the bathroom. The ceilings are vaulted to the roof with a loft space over the bedrooms.

"Damn, dude, this is nice!" Max steps inside with his mouth hanging open and wide eyes.

I chuckle. "You already said that."

"But I mean it."

There's a beat-up love seat against one wall and my grandmother's old rocking chair in the corner, both pointed at the TV. There are three barstools by the counter that were there when I moved in.

"I guess the landlord just finished a renovation. The yard is still kind of a mess in the back. The pool is all murky, so I wouldn't go in there, but the house is nice." I watch as he moves into the kitchen and looks out the back window. I point to the hallway to the left of the front of the house. "The bedrooms are through there. Yours would be the one in the back."

He steps around the corner into the empty second bedroom. "Decent size. Much bigger than my room now."

"Just as long as it's not a mess by time we move out at the end of the summer."

He looks over at me. "You're not staying?"

I shake my head. "Not unless I find a job down here."

"Which is unlikely."

I shrug. "It could happen."

"In your dreams."

"Well, it's a month-to-month lease, so we can see where we're at later. But what do you say? Does this work for you?"

He laughs and shakes my hand. "Yeah, man. This works for me. When can I move in?"

Chapter Three:

Robyn

I take a sip of my crappy home-brewed coffee as I make my way down First Street. It's opening day for the Pier and it's early. The sun is just rising over the ocean and I can see the silhouette of my best friend Jessie running on the beach.

She and her grandma run Montana Manor, which is the only inn in town. She always wakes up super early to run and I admire her for it, but I don't have time for that. I have things to do and places to be. Besides, I work on my feet most of the day. I get my exercise in.

The coffee shop is just opening up when I walk by. I wave to Nancy through the window, but keep on walking. I don't have time to stop. I didn't even work on my painting at all this morning. I'm too focused on the Pier today. It's taken some nagging, but my team and I finally got it all cleaned up and ready for customers this past week. Still, there's some office work that I need to do before the day gets started, so I want to get there early.

At the office, I flick on the light and hit the power button for the computer. Spinning in my chair, I check the schedule for today on the cork board behind my desk as I wait for it to warm up. Peggy and Max are both working today. Not my favorite, but Peggy needs to be here because she's my assistant and it's opening day and, whether I like it or not, Max has been here the longest, which means I can count on him to get things done.

When he shows up.

I notice that Jaden is also working today. I had Mackenzie show him how to run the rides and no matter what ride I put him on, he seemed to pick it up right away. Plus, he's been a big help this past week with everything else. I'm curious to see how he and the other new people do now that the park's open.

Once the computer is up and running, I look at some of the stats from the last several years. Slowly, the numbers on opening day are decreasing, although the money made each season has increased. Rising ticket prices and more money spent at concessions helped with that. Not to mention, we got a fairly-popular comedian from North Beach to come and do a show here last summer, which drew a large crowd. He was booked already for this year, so we won't have him. We have half the season booked, but no one as popular as he was.

I crunch some numbers and figure we'll have to have even more people this year than last year if we want to meet our financial goals. I don't like trying to estimate concession sales because that's usually pretty dependent on the weather. If it's really sunny, more people buy drinks. If it's cloudy, less drinks sold. I guess the same can be said about ticket sales, though.

The business is still profitable, but not by a lot. Nobody's getting rich off the Montana Beach Pier. It makes me wonder how many more years we'll be open. If the owner decides his money is better spent elsewhere, we're stuck because nobody who truly cares for the Pier has enough to keep it open. We just need to keep things going for as long as possible.

Summer Job

"Am I too early?"

I jump and bump my coffee. It spills all over my desk onto the floor.

"I'm sorry!" Jaden rushes forward to help me move the papers away. "I didn't mean to scare you."

"It's okay," I mutter. "I must've been zoning out. Here, let me get some paper towels." I hurry into the break room and grab the whole roll.

He holds up some of the soggy papers from my desk. "I hope none of this was too important."

I rip off several sheets from the roll and start wiping up the floor. "Nothing that can't be printed again, I suppose."

"What is all this stuff?" he asks, patting at the papers with a wad of paper towels.

"Just some attendance projections."

"Like customers?"

"Yeah."

"Does it sound promising?"

I shrug.

"Oh."

I glance up at him and toss the soiled paper towels in the trash. "Not horrible. You're not going to find yourself unemployed in the middle of the summer, but things could be better."

"I see, yeah. I was talking to Max the other day and he said that the Pier is actually one of the only attractions left in Montana Beach." He wipes up what's left of the coffee from the desk.

"Besides the beach," I add. I'm surprised that Max would give any sort of compliment to this place, but then, there has to be a reason he keeps coming back. He can't hate it here—or me—*that* much.

"That's kind of sad," Jaden says. "It's nice here."

With the floor wiped up, I take my seat again and help him dab at the papers. "Well, I'm glad you like it. Have you been exploring the town much?"

"Not really because we've been working so much. I went to the beach the other day when I had off. It's quiet. I liked it."

"That's good. Yeah, sorry about having you jump in full time right away. We kind of need all hands on deck at the start of the season."

"No worries." He tosses more wet paper towels in the trash and gathers the dried papers. "So this place really isn't doing too hot?"

"I'm probably just overreacting." I try to downplay it. It's probably not a good idea to get the employees worried. "Don't go spreading it around that things are bad."

He takes a seat in the chair across from me and shakes his head. "I won't. Is there anything I can do to help?"

"You mean *not* make me spill my coffee?" I smirk.

His face darkens a little. "Sorry again."

"Don't worry about it. But as far as what you can do, really the biggest thing is to just help keep the rest of the staff in line. Everyone hates me because I'm the only one calling them out for being lazy. The last manager just let everyone do whatever. That's probably why he got fired. Anyway, since I've been promoted, they haven't liked me."

He scratches behind his ear and looks at the floor. "Yeah, I kind of got that impression."

I open my mouth to respond, but I hear the door open into the break room and Peggy steps in.

"I'll go out and start sweeping," Jaden says quickly.

"Good idea. Thanks."

He's out the door before Peggy comes into the office.

§ § §

TO MY SURPRISE, there are more customers at the Pier than I thought there would be. The only real hiccup to the day is having to cover for Max's tardiness. He finally strolled in half an hour after we opened, which was a full hour after he was scheduled to be here. Luckily, since he's a cleaner, there wasn't a lot to clean first thing in the morning, but I'm still not happy about it. But, if that's the only real issue on opening day, I'm a good with that. It's not like I wasn't expecting it anyway.

By the time I check the day's numbers at closing, I'm very happy to see that there were more people this year than last year. It's always hard to tell what marketing efforts helped bring more people through the doors, but I'll definitely have to do some investigating tomorrow.

I count out the day's money and enter it into the computer separated by concessions and ticket sales. By the time I'm done, I have a big pile of cash sitting on the desk that needs to be verified by someone else, but everyone's cleared out for the day. After the sound of kids giggling and screaming all day long, it's weird for there to be complete silence in the office.

Peggy's supposed to stay with me to help me close, but she took off early because her son had a doctor's appointment. Valid excuse, I suppose. I just wish she had scheduled it for another day, but I guess you can't always choose.

I was so busy in the shuffle that I forgot to ask Max to stay. Besides Peggy, he's the next logical choice to help me count out the day's money and make sure the Pier is in tip-top shape for tomorrow's opening. Based purely on seniority, obviously. He took off as soon as seven o'clock hit and the park officially closed. Wouldn't want to spend an extra minute here.

I look out the window and see Jaden putting a garbage bag in one of the cans by the gates. I'm surprised he's still here since everyone else went home. Either way, I'm glad he is because now I can close out everything tonight instead of rushing through it tomorrow morning.

I pop my head out the door and ask, “Hey, can you come in here and help me for a sec?”

“Uh, sure.” He follows me into the office and takes a seat across from the desk. “I know my shift ended at seven, and if you don’t want to pay me for the time after, I understand. I just wanted to get a few extra things done before I left. I figured it’d be less to do tomorrow.”

I smile. “No, that’s fine. Actually, I was really happy to see that. Thanks.” Hopefully his work ethic will rub off on the rest of the workers.

“No problem,” he says. “Just doing my part.”

“Well, thank you.” I sit back and smile at him. He’s so nice and his smile makes me do the same and I could just—

“So…what did you need help with?” he asks.

“Oh!” I grab the wad of cash and pause. “How good are you at counting money?”

“Well, I’ve had some retail experience—”

“Oh, right! Well, I just need you to count this so we can verify the amount and I can close everything out for tonight.” I set the stack on the desk in front of him and pass him a calculator. “I’m sure you’ve done this before, but I like to count out each hundred and then add that in the calculator, but you can do whatever method works for you. As long as we get the same number, it doesn’t really matter.” I turn back to the computer and click around, trying to pretend that I wasn’t just staring at him.

“Sure thing.” He grabs the bills and counts it out quick, like someone who’s worked with cash before.

When he’s done, he tells me the total, which matches mine, and I plug it into the computer to finish closing everything for the day.

“You can go if you want,” I tell him as I stuff the money into the deposit bag. “I’m sure you’re getting hungry.”

He shakes his head. "No, that's okay. I wouldn't feel comfortable leaving you to walk home alone. It's a small town, but you never know."

I bite my top lip to try to hide my smile, but I probably just come off as a freak. Eh, what else is new? Everyone here hates me already anyway.

Well, everyone except for Jaden.

Once I've finished everything and have turned the computer off, I grab my bag and lead Jaden out of the building, making sure to lock the door behind us.

"Thanks again for all your hard work," I say as we start walking down Ocean Boulevard. "Not just today, but all week. Someone like you is just what we needed around here."

"No problem, ma'am, just—"

I stop walking and grab his arm. "Okay, first of all, don't call me *ma'am*. I'm probably not that much older than you. I may be your boss, but I'm not your mother. Just call me Robyn."

He looks scared and nods quickly.

I laugh. "Sorry, but it just sounded weird. No, definitely call me Robyn."

"Okay." He nods again and then adds, "Robyn."

I start walking again. "Just keep saying it. You'll get used to it."

He chuckles. "Okay, Robyn."

"You said you live on Cemetery Street?"

"Yup. Hey, you remembered."

"Well, after forgetting so much of your history, I'm determined to remember *something*." We turn onto Third Street.

"So you remembered where I live? That seems…creepy." He smiles to show he's joking.

"It's a small town, everyone knows everyone's secrets here. Especially the newbies."

"Guess I better get used to it, then."

"So how was your first day?" I ask. "Well, your first day with the park opened."

Jaden lets out a deep breath. "Busy, just like everyone said it would be."

I chuckle. "Ready for another tomorrow?"

"I need a good night's sleep. Between the sun and being on my feet, I'm wiped."

"Yeah, it can be tiring, but that's part of the reason I love it," I say. "You'll get used to it, too."

"Yeah."

We're quiet as we cross over Montana Boulevard and I turn right, toward Fourth Street—my street.

"How has everyone been treating you?" I ask him.

"Good. They all seem nice, for the most part."

"Don't let them see you with me, then." I laugh.

"Yeah, they definitely don't like you."

"No need to sugarcoat it, then!"

He smiles. "Sorry, but you even said it yourself."

"Yeah," I say with a sigh. "And I don't care *that* much if they like me, I just wish they would respect me and they don't. I mean, look at the way Max was late today. The gates were open before he got there. He's supposed to be there half an hour before we open to get everything in order."

"But what kind of consequence is there for coming in late?" Jaden asks. "Maybe nobody's really afraid of being late because they know nothing's going to happen. They just think you're annoying."

"Oh, thanks!" We turn onto my street.

He chuckles. "I'm just saying, there needs to be consequences when people break the rules."

I nod. "Well, I've been thinking about implementing a point system that tallies up when people are late, but I haven't really fleshed out the details yet."

"So do it. There will be growing pains, of course, but you need to make them afraid of you a little bit."

"Yeah, maybe. I'll come up with something." I slow down in front of my house. "This is me."

It's a little two-story house. Blue, like a lot of the houses in town, with white trim work. There's a palm tree in the front yard near the white picket fence that has chipped paint and there's a small flower garden under the bay window in the front of the house. The porch swing sways in the slight breeze by the red front door.

He nods. "Nice place."

"Thanks. And thanks for walking me home." I look down at the broken sidewalk and then up at the house. "Well, I guess I'll see you tomorrow, then."

"Yeah, definitely," he says. "I can even stay late again if you want."

"That'd be nice, yeah. You definitely counted the money faster than Peggy."

"It's not hard."

"No, it's not." I shove my hands in my pockets. "Well, good night."

"Night." He slowly turns and continues down the street. I watch him until he reaches the end and turns right.

What is it about that boy that makes me want to linger like this?

Chapter Four:

Jaden

At the counter in the kitchen, I start to gather my things to head to work when Max comes out of his room. He's wearing a pair of gym shorts and scratches at his bare chest as he stumbles over to the refrigerator. Pretty comfortable for his first week living with someone he just met.

"Are you working today?" I ask.

He yawns and stretches. "Yeah."

I nod to the clock on the stove. "It's getting late. You should hurry."

He grabs a box of cereal from the cupboard—my cereal. He hasn't chipped in for any groceries yet. "Meh, I'm not worried about it. I'll get there when I get there."

My conversation with Robyn last night rings in my head. I wonder if she's going to actually start buckling down on attendance and punctuality or if that was just talk. Either way, I tell Max, "You should still try to hurry."

"You don't have to wait for me." He takes a seat at the

breakfast bar and pours milk into his bowl.

I hesitate and consider telling him that Robyn's getting serious about being to work on time. Not to mention the fact that she called him out by name, but that would tell him that I talked to her. It would invite more questions and could potentially reveal that I walked her home last night. It would make for a miserable summer if my coworkers stopped talking to me because I'm cozying up with the boss.

Not that I would mind seeing more of Robyn, that is.

Instead, I just say, "Okay fine. But I'm not going to cover for you if she asks."

"Just tell her I overslept. I'm not worried about it."

"If you say so. Maybe I'll see you later."

I head down Cemetery Street to First Street and take that all the way across town to the Pier. A part of me wants to walk by Robyn's house to see if I can catch her on her way in, but I decide that's probably not a good idea. I would come off as a creep, which is exactly the opposite of what I want. I was so worried about what Max would think of me if he knew I had had a conversation with her before. I should just go solo today.

It's a beautiful morning and the sun feels nice as I walk to work. I'm happy I decided to move to Montana Beach this summer. But, if I'm being honest with myself, the reason I'm most excited to get to work is to see Robyn. I haven't stopped thinking about her since last night. She just seems so genuine. So relatable. I want to spend more time with her, which is weird because she's my boss.

At work, it's as if my wish has come true: Robyn's the only one here so far.

"Oh good, I was hoping you'd be early again." She marches toward me at my locker from the office with a paper in her hand.

"Morning." I stuff my bag in my locker and pull out my

water bottle, trying to play off the fact that I like it that she was thinking about me.

"Morning," she says quickly with a smile. "Sorry, I've been here for a bit and have had like three cups of coffee, so I'm kind of wired."

I laugh. "Sounds like you've had a busy morning."

"A very productive one," she adds. "Between last night and today, I've come up with a point system for attendance that I'm going to implement today."

"Gotcha." I wonder how mad Max is going to be when he hears about this.

"I know there's going to be pushback," she continues.

"Yeah, probably."

"No, there definitely will be. I can name several people who are going to have to change their habits around here if they want to keep their jobs. They're going to be pissed and I was hoping you could help me with that."

Oh. So that's why she was hoping I'd be here early.

"How?" I ask.

"Back me up, if you could." Her beautiful hazel eyes meet mine and beg me to say yes.

"How am I—I'm just the new guy. Nobody's going to listen to me."

She shakes her head. "I don't know if I agree with that. Lots of people like you, that's why I'm coming to you."

"Uh…"

"I'm not saying you need to hype everyone up when I break the news at this morning's meeting, but maybe throughout the day if you hear people talking, just say how it's not a bad idea or whatever—unless you think it *is* a bad idea?"

I shake my head quickly. "No, it's perfect. I told you that last night. I just—" Her eyes plead with me again and I cave. "Yeah, I'll do what I can."

Robyn smiles widely. "Yes! Thank you so much!" She jumps and gives me a hug, releasing me immediately. "Sorry. That was, uh—"

"It's okay," I blurt.

Her cheeks darken. "I'm going to go, uh, look for any loopholes before everyone—"

"What loopholes?" Peggy slides her bug-eye sunglasses to the top of her head as she steps into the break room snapping her gum and hauling an oversized purse.

"Oh good, you're here too," Robyn says with less enthusiasm. "Come on in the office, I want to run something by you real quick."

They disappear in the office and I pull out my phone and scroll through today's news feed as some of my coworkers start to arrive. Within fifteen minutes, the room is filled.

Robyn and Peggy step out of the office, one clearly happier than the other, and stand at the front of the room.

"Is everyone here?" Robyn asks. "I want to talk to you guys about something before we get started for the day."

"Max isn't here," Peggy says after counting everyone.

Robyn looks around. "I guess he isn't. Well, I'll fill him in later. Anyway, each year I try to make a list of goals that we can accomplish to become better workers and provide a better experience for our guests. The big thing I think we really need to tackle this year is attendance."

Several people groan.

She ignores them. "For the most part, you're all hard workers once you're here…but getting in the door can be a challenge sometimes. Trust me, I know."

"We're here now," Mackenzie says to my right.

"I see that, yeah," Robyn says with a nod. "But previous experience has shown that attendance drops as the summer goes on. This new system I've come up with will hopefully keep everyone in check. If one of us isn't here, then the rest of us need to pick up the slack and we might lose out on an opportunity to make a guest's day extra-special."

I let out a deep breath, feeling secondhand embarrassment for her. She's trying too hard to be nice and people aren't really listening.

"Okay, so the system I've come up with is pretty easy. It's like baseball with a three-strike rule—"

Everyone's attention turns to the door as Max walks in. I'm actually surprised he's here so early. I really thought the park would be open before he strolled in, just like it was yesterday.

"You're late, Max," Robyn says.

He shrugs.

"This is actually pretty fitting because we were just talking about new rules for attendance."

"I'm here. I'm attending, aren't I?" he says.

"But you're late."

He smirks. "But I'm here."

Several people laugh, but Robyn gives him a stern look until he takes a seat.

"Anyway," she continues with a little less cheer. "It's a simple three-point system. For each time you don't show up to work, you get a strike. By the third strike, you're fired. If you're late, you get a late strike and for every three late strikes, it equals one no-show strike. Got it?"

Most of the room grumbles.

Max raises his hand and I cringe, knowing it can't end well. He can be a nice guy, but he's an ass to Robyn. I wonder if it's just because he has an audience.

"I have a question," he says.

Robyn takes a deep breath. "What is it?"

"What if we don't want to listen to your new rule?"

"You don't really have a choice."

"What are you going to do if we don't listen?"

Her eyes narrow. "Was there a part you didn't understand? By the third strike, you're fired. It's simple enough."

"Ah, but what if we show up to work anyway?"

"Then you'd be wasting your time because you wouldn't be getting paid," she says. "I'd have to call security and have you—I mean, *that person*—escorted from the grounds."

"What if we show up as a guest?" he pushes.

Robyn glances at Peggy, who's fussing with her nails.

"Listen to Robyn, guys," she says like she's bored.

"This rule is stupid," Max adds.

With Peggy's halfhearted attempt having failed, Robyn looks to me for help.

"Look guys," I speak up, "she's not asking for a lot. Nothing's going to change if we just do our jobs and show up when we're supposed to."

My heart races as I see almost everyone glower at me, but they all look away when Robyn starts again.

"Jaden's right. Most of you don't have anything to worry about. And if you need something changed on the schedule, just let me know ahead of time and we can make it work. Now, it's getting late. If there aren't any other questions, let's head out and start opening things for the day."

Someone by the door gets to his feet and walks out, followed by Peggy and the rest of the room. I catch Robyn's eyes and she mouths a thank you. I give her a nod.

As the day goes on, though, I feel the repercussions of what I said as nobody—not even Max, really—talks to me more than they have to. Other than the standard "All clear!" signal or "Closing time!" call, I don't talk to any of my coworkers, who all quickly file out of the park at closing. I can only imagine how it'd be if they knew I walked Robyn home last night.

"So how bad was it today after you stood up for me this

morning?" Robyn asks as I count out the money in the office.

I don't know if Robyn sent Peggy home or if she was just as annoyed by the new three-strike point system, but it's just me and Robyn again tonight. I'm not complaining. It's what I was hoping for when I told her I could stay late.

"Not terrible," I say. "For one day, at least."

She scrunches her nose. "Sorry about that. What you said was perfect, though. Hopefully it makes a difference."

"Yeah."

It's quiet for a moment as I sift through the bills, my lips moving as I count.

"Are you feeling more comfortable about your job?" she asks.

"It's not too bad. The guests can be fun. Some of those control rooms are stuffy in the heat, though."

"Yeah, I know. The AC's broken. That's the lack of funding I was talking about. I don't think the owners have ever been here to see how dated this place is."

"It's not too bad if you open a window," I add.

She grins. "It's not even July yet."

I finish counting and set the stack of money back in front of her and tell her the total.

"Perfect!" she says, turning back to the computer. "Let me just punch a couple numbers in and we'll be on our way."

I notice how she doesn't tell me I can leave before her. Maybe she wants to walk home with me too. Or maybe that's just wishful thinking.

In the break room, I gather my things as Robyn closes out the park on the computer for the night.

"Ready?" she asks with a bag slung over her shoulder.

"Yup." I step outside and wait for her to lock the door before we head out. Over the town, the sun sets on the horizon.

"It's beautiful," I say. "The sunsets are my favorite part about this place."

She looks at me. "Never gets old."

Turning to her, I notice how the light reflects in her hazel eyes. They're captivating. Just like her.

"What?" She looks down at herself and then wipes at her face. "Am I grimy from sweat?" She lifts her arm and sniffs.

I chuckle. "No, your eyes are just beautiful."

An involuntary grin spreads across her face and she drops her arm. "Oh. Thanks."

Chewing on my bottom lip, I turn away so I don't make her uncomfortable by staring at her. Still, I wish I could steal another few seconds looking into those eyes.

"We should get going," she says.

The downtown area of First Street is filled with buildings you'd never find in North Beach. Not anymore, at least. They were all torn down for gas stations, hotels, and condos. These old buildings, even if a lot of them are empty, are part of what makes Montana Beach special.

And Robyn. I wouldn't enjoy it here nearly as much without her.

"I want to thank you again for sticking up for me," she says once we cross Montana Boulevard. "It meant a lot to me for someone to have my back for a change."

I'm quiet for a moment as I wrestle with myself over what my next words will be. Finally, I decide to throw caution to the wind and say what's on my mind.

"You could thank me by going out with me sometime."

As soon as the words leave my lips, I regret them. What a line. Robyn's not some college girl looking for a good time. She's different.

"Not like a date-date—maybe just like a bar, what's that one next to the Pier?" I add quickly.

"The Nine?"

"Yeah! We could hang out there. Or, I don't know, even just

get like, I don't know, ice cream or something." Wow. Really lame. I've never invited a girl on an *ice cream* date.

"Or not," I say. "It's fine if you're not interested. I just thought…" I trail off, not wanting to say what I actually thought. What I'd hoped.

Robyn lets out a deep breath. "Jaden, I'm just not sure if it's a good idea. You're several years younger than me—not that that is a deal breaker, but, I don't know, I'm your boss…"

"Yeah." I nod quickly. "No, that makes sense. That's fine."

She shakes her head. "No, it's not." A nervous laugh escapes her. "Forget what I just said. I like spending time with you and I'd like to spend more."

I suddenly realize we're at her house already. I wish this town was bigger only so we could have more time to talk like this. But then, I *did* just ask her out and she might not be saying no…

"So…"

She smiles. "Yes. I'd love to go out with you sometime."

Chapter Five:

Robyn

"Ahh!" Nancy's granddaughters Olivia and Ava scream as they loop around on the ladybug ride.

Nancy and I are standing against the fence and she's snapping pictures with her phone.

"They sound like they're having fun," I say.

"Oh, they're having the best time!" Nancy says. "I love it that we have something like this right in town."

"So do I."

The Pier is filled with kids and I have a million things to check up on but I wanted to spend some time with Nancy because she seemed really excited to bring her granddaughters the last time I stopped into the coffee shop.

She brought them for Boris the Brute. He's a comedian who puts on a whole show that revolves around him being clumsy and silly. It's corny, but the kids really loved it last year, so I invited him back.

The girls come through the gate laughing.

"Grandma! Grandma! Did you see how fast we were going?" Olivia shouts. Her dark hair is in braids tied with baby blue beads.

They can't be more than five or six, so the Pier must seem huge to them. I smile and hope that they continue to have that sense of wonder for as long as possible.

"I did, yeah," Nancy says. "You guys weren't scared at all?"

"Nope, not one bit!" Ava says. She's younger and has tripped more than once with her pink Barbie flip flops.

"You're so brave!"

"Can we go on the Ferris wheel?" Olivia asks.

"I think the show's starting soon," I tell them. "You want to make sure you get a good seat. The Ferris wheel will still be here when it's over."

The girls take Nancy's hands and pull her off toward the stage.

Nancy giggles and says, "I guess we're going to the show now!"

I smile and watch them leave.

"Slacking on the job?"

I jump and turn to see Jaden laughing.

"You did that on purpose!"

He smiles. "I did nothing of the sort."

"Besides, shouldn't *you* be working? I hear your boss is a bitch."

He shrugs. "Eh, you gotta know how to schmooze her."

"Oh, it's that easy, is it?"

"I'm learning the best way to sweet talk her."

"Ah, you think you're pretty slick, huh?"

"I guess we'll find out later tonight." He walks toward the break room after flashing me another winning smile.

I watch him walk away and smile like a dope. What am I getting into with him?

§ § §

"SO WHERE DO you want to go on our date?" Jaden asks freely once everyone's left for the day. We're in the office and I'm finishing up today's deposit for the bank.

I've been thinking about our date a lot since he asked me out last night. It makes me nervous to cross that line, but I really like him. First thing this morning he asked me the same question: where are we going? I told him I needed the day to consider it, but I've been preoccupied with work—and just the idea of the date—to give much thought to here we should go.

"Or would you rather wait? Or not go at all?" he asks in my silence.

I shake my head. "No, I definitely want to go."

His face lights up. "Good."

"I'm just still—"

"Not sure where to go?" he finishes.

I slip the wad of cash in the deposit envelope and toss it in the safe. "What about ice cream?"

His smile is perfect. "Ice cream? That's what you want? I was kind of kidding when I suggested that..."

"So you don't want to go on an ice cream date with me?" I hit the power button on the computer and gather my things.

"I didn't say that."

"You basically said it."

He follows me out into the break room, where he grabs his own bag. "Okay. Ice cream it is. When?"

"Now." Holding the door open for him, I wait for him to step through but he stops in his tracks.

"Now?"

"Do you have other plans?"

Jaden steps out of the way so I can close the door. "Well...no, I just thought..." He lifts his collar over his nose and sniffs. "I just thought I'd be a little less sweaty when we go."

I laugh. "I'm sweaty too. Hence, the ice cream." With the door properly locked, I turn back to him and smile. "Ready?"

"Those eyes." He shakes his head and smiles. "They were made for the sunset."

Smiling, I turn away from the Pier and down First Street.

"I think we need to set some ground rules first," I say as we walk.

"Like what?"

"Like this is just one date for now. We'll see how it feels afterwards."

He nods. "Yeah, of course."

"And this won't change things at work," I continue. "I still need to be your boss first and foremost."

"Yes, ma'am—oh, sorry. Yes, *Robyn*."

I smile.

"Can I add something?"

I look at him suspiciously. "Okay..."

"Even if we don't continue any sort of romantic relationship, I still want to be able to walk you home after work," he says. "This is a safe town, but you still shouldn't be alone. Besides, I like your company."

My smile is still spread across my face. "You're sweet. Sure, that sounds fair."

We order our ice creams—Jaden a soft twist, me double chocolate chunk—and take them out to the park next door to eat them in the setting sun. It's a tiny little pocket park, situated at the corner of Montana Boulevard and First Street. It's across from Montana Manor and right next to the beach, so it's a pretty popular spot in the day time. It's the closest place to the beach that has shade thanks to the large oak tree in the middle.

Jaden and I sit at a picnic table under the tree. He watches the waves, I watch the people walking on the sidewalk along

First Street. We're quiet, but neither of us seems to mind.

"I haven't had ice cream in a long time," I finally say.

"I think it was sixth grade the last time I had it."

"*Sixth grade*?" I nearly shout, as if he said he doesn't believe in gravity or something.

He chuckles. "Mind-blowing, I know."

I laugh at my own reaction. "I would've thought with you living in North Beach that you would have it all the time."

"My freezer's usually filled with popsicles—or I get a slushie from the 7-Eleven down the street from my parents."

I make a face. "Both of those are just frozen Kool-Aid."

"But so delicious."

"Not as good as ice cream." I lick up the drippy parts around the side of my cone.

"I can tell," he says with a chuckle. "You've got chocolate all over your face."

"I do?" I wipe at my mouth, feeling my face flush with embarrassment. I didn't care what he thought when I ordered the most loaded ice cream available, but I didn't think I'd be *wearing* it. "Did I get it?"

"Here." He takes a clean napkin and reaches across the table to wipe my face.

In an effort not to stare at him cross-eyed, I look back to the street and see Peggy and her husband step into the diner. I pull away from Jaden and duck down behind the table to hide, dropping my cone to the ground as I do.

"What?" Jaden asks.

It hits me how ridiculous I look and I sit up. "Sorry. I just thought someone saw me."

He turns and tries to spot what I was looking at. "So what if someone saw you?"

"It was Peggy," I say, as if that explains everything.

"So?"

I shrug.

He looks annoyed. "Are you embarrassed to be seen with me?"

"No, I'm not—I just thought—Jaden, you understand, don't you?"

His look is still hard. "No. I don't, actually."

I look toward the diner again. "It's just...weird."

"Weird..." He nods slowly.

"It's just different. I'm having a good time."

"Really? Is that why you keep checking to see if she's looking this way?"

"Jaden, I'm sorry. It's not—I just..." I let out a heavy sigh. "It's probably better if we don't mix work and...outside-of-work." No way was I going to say "pleasure." This is certainly not pleasure.

He narrows his eyes. "So what are you saying?"

"It's probably better if we only see each other at work."

Nodding, he gets up and tosses his cone in the trash can by the street corner.

"Jaden, it's not that I don't like you—"

He jogs to cross the street. I consider following him, but I hear my phone ding in my pocket. It's a text from Jessie.

It's been a crappy night already. I have food for two and no one to share it with. Want to come over?

Sounds like my night. I look down the street to where Jaden's marching away. He's too mad to talk anymore tonight. And I don't even know what I'd say.

Another ding.

Oh, and bring wine.

I swipe to reply and type, *Yeah, I'll be over in a bit.*

§ § §

"THAT WAS GOOD, Jessie, thanks." I sit back in the chair and clutch at my full belly. An empty plate that earlier had spaghetti on it sits in front of me on the table. "Just what I needed: comfort food and alcohol."

"Are you going to elaborate on why you needed it?" She sips the last of her wine. It was the last bottle she had in the apartment she shares with her grandma on the third floor of the Manor. The wine I brought still sits on the table between our plates.

"Are you going to elaborate on why it's been a crappy night?" I counter.

She chews on the inside of her cheek for a moment and then grabs the bottle on the table. "Let's crack this open too."

I carry our plates over to the sink as she works the cork out of the bottle.

"That stressful of a day, huh?" I ask.

"No, today was great. This evening is what sucked." The bottle goes *pop* as she yanks the cork out.

"Why's that?"

Jessie fills two glasses and takes a sip of hers before responding. "Let's see, I told my grandma how everything she and my grandpa have ever worked for could be taken away from us without our say. Oh, and I just got ditched on a date."

She told me earlier that a developer wants to buy Montana Manor to build a hotel tower. Jessie and one of her guests, Mason, went around the last few days getting people to sign a petition and to invite them to a Fourth of July party at the Manor. Beyond that, she wouldn't tell me much more about Mason, but I know there's more to their story.

I make a face. "I'm sorry. I know this isn't what you want to hear, but I think you just need to have patience with the Manor. You've done all you can for today. Tomorrow you'll do more to make the party a success."

"Yeah, you're probably right."

I sip my wine and hope that she'll voluntarily tell me about Mason. When she doesn't, I ask, "So…you had a date?"

"I was *supposed* to. Maybe. More like a thank you dinner. I don't know. It didn't happen, regardless."

"Did he give a reason?" I ask.

"Not really."

"Well, at least you didn't have a chance to royally mess it up like I did."

"What do you mean?" she asks.

"I kind of had a date earlier, too."

"When I texted you? You could've told me you were busy!"

I move to the balcony patio overlooking the ocean. "Well, him storming off because I made an ass of myself was kind of a big sign that the date had ended."

Jessie takes the seat beside me. "What did you do? Who is this guy? You haven't said anything about him."

"Well, that's the thing. He's, uh—he works at the Pier."

"Like a maintenance guy?"

I shake my head.

"Robyn, don't tell me he's your *employee*!"

I cringe. "I know, it's bad. I shouldn't get involved with him, but Jessie, if you knew him you'd be going after him too. Besides, how is it any different than you dating one of your guests?"

She turns away. "Completely different."

I giggle. "Sure."

"So what's his name?"

"Jaden."

"And why did he storm off?"

"I thought I saw someone else from work and I hid."

"Smooth."

I put up my hand in surrender. "I know, it wasn't my finest moment."

"What did he say?"

"He thinks I'm embarrassed by him, which isn't *exactly* true. I just don't want to get fired."

"What do you mean it isn't *exactly* true?"

"He's quite a bit younger." I look over to see the disgust on her face. "Not *that* young. I think he's like twenty-two, but I can't exactly ask that because, you know, I'm his *employer*." I wipe at my face, sticky with sweat. "Oh God, what am I doing with him?"

Jessie smiles. "You like him, there's nothing wrong with that. But maybe you should hold off on doing anything about it until he's not your employee anymore."

I sigh. "Yeah, maybe."

"You don't seem to like that option."

"Not really, no." I laugh.

"Have you…?"

"No! Have you? With Mason?"

She shakes her head. "No, just kissed."

"Oh?"

"At the park in the grass. I was holding yogurt."

"Is that a euphemism?"

She laughs. "No!"

I sit back and sip my wine. "I miss this. It's been a while since we've had a girl's night."

"Yeah, we were long overdue."

"We should go out," I suggest.

"Sure. When? I'm going to be a little busy the next week or so planning for this party."

"Tonight."

"Tonight?" she yelps.

"Yeah, let's go!"

Jessie looks over at me, unsure. "Shouldn't you shower first?"

"I suppose, but I can do that here. If you don't mind. Also, I'd need to borrow some clothes."

She laughs. "Oh, I see how it is! Like your closet isn't big enough?"

I roll my eyes. "You mean the one that's taking over my art studio? We're not talking about that. We're talking about tonight. Are we going or not?"

"I'd rather not."

"But you will?" I ask with a smirk. "Come on, it'll be fun. Just for a little bit. We can go to the Nine and see if the guys are working."

"So much for our girl's night." She sets her glass on the table and sits up. Now I've got her. "Fine, but just for a little while. Let me get you something to wear."

I raise my hands and cheer. I down the rest of my glass and head inside to shower and get ready.

Within forty-five minutes, we're all cleaned up, dolled up, and walking down to the Nine, the closest thing we have to a club in town. It doesn't hurt that our other two best friends, Adrian and Tyler, work there.

"We're leaving by one," Jessie says as she readjusts her top.

"We'll see," I respond.

It takes us a minute to get through the door. That's a good sign for business, but annoying as we try to navigate the brick staircase leading to the basement bar.

"Drinks first?" I ask Jessie, but she moves quickly through the crowd toward a couple by the bar.

I get stuck behind a group of girls dancing around the tables for the restaurant and only get around them in time to see Jessie slap a blond guy across the face. As she marches back toward the door, she looks like she's about to cry.

Now I feel guilty for insisting we come.

Turning, I quickly follow her back out onto the sidewalk.

"Jessie, are you okay?" I ask.

"What an ass," she mutters. "You think you know someone."

"Wait, was that Mason?"

"Yes."

"Jessie!" His voice calls from behind us. He jogs to catch up and grabs Jessie's shoulder to stop her.

I shoot him a warning look.

She spins around and shouts, "Stay away from me!"

"What's the matter?" he asks, but she turns to continue back to the Manor. "Jessie, I didn't do anything wrong!"

She stops in her tracks and turns on him, accuses him of seeing another girl while seeing her. Mason insists it wasn't what it looked like.

Even though Jessie's my best friend, I can't help but feel like she's quick to assume the worst of Mason. She's not even trying to hear his side of the story. It reminds me of what happened earlier between me and Jaden. Only, I'm like Mason in that situation.

I try to pull Jessie back to the Manor. She just needs to forget about all of this for now. Wait until she cools down before she talks to him again. She doesn't listen to me, though. Too focused on her argument with Mason.

She wipes away the tears pooling from her eyes, her voice defeated. "Do you even know why I moved back home?"

He shrugs. "I don't know, your grandma's dying business?"

Ouch. Not good, Mason. Not good at all.

He recognizes his mistake and quickly adds, "Jess, I didn't—"

"I found out my fiancé was cheating on me."

Ah, so that's what this is. I forgot about that. Suddenly, it all makes sense now.

A silence falls between them.

"Oh," he finally says.

Jessie wipes at her eyes again. "Yeah. So pardon me if seeing you with another girl is triggering for me."

"I'm sorry that happened to you, but that's not what's going on here," he says.

"Come on, Robyn, let's go." She turns back and starts marching back toward the Manor.

I hurry to keep up and hear Mason following behind us.

"Jessie, you're the reason I canceled our plans."

"Oh, that's great." Jessie continues her power-walk without even a glance back. That's good. As long as she doesn't—

"Decided you no longer liked me, huh?" she adds. "Or maybe it suddenly hit you that you've been leading me on."

I wish she would stop talking to him. Just drop it for now.

"No, it's not like that," he says. "You're—you got in my head. You're confusing me. This decision I have to make is even more impossible than it was before."

What decision?

"You're going to do what you want anyway," she says. "Just leave me alone until you leave and we'll be good, okay? I'll get over it. I have before."

Mason stops following us and we keep power-walking back to the Manor. A million thoughts fly through my head the whole time, comparing Jessie's situation to mine and Jaden's.

It's clear they want to be together, sure, but they're both so guarded that they're not truly letting each other in. Is that how I am with Jaden? Am I pushing him away in order to protect myself? That's sure what it seems like.

I love Jessie, but she's standing in her own way from letting Mason into her life—someone who could make her very happy. I don't want to be like that. I don't want to act in fear of getting hurt. Like I did with Jaden today. Things are going to be different for us.

I like him.

I want to see him.

I need to apologize.

Chapter Six:

Jaden

I'm in charge of the Ferris wheel today. The sun is extra hot and the control room is stuffy even with the windows open. I'm sweating out bottles of water faster than I can drink them.

Robyn wants to make sure that we drink a lot today. She and Peggy have been walking around passing out cold bottles of water to everyone who's working. We're also operating on a shorter rotation cycle so we can escape to the break room more often. Not that the AC in there is the best, but at least it's something.

Luckily, Peggy's been the one to drop off my water all day, so I don't need to see Robyn. I haven't talked to her much since our ill-fated date last week. Peggy's been staying after work to help her close—like it should be, technically—and I've been hanging back and walking to work with Max in the mornings. He's actually been on time all week. Looks like the point system is working.

When the Ferris wheel comes to a stop so people can get on,

I take the opportunity to drink more water. The bottle's empty, though.

"Damn," I mutter to myself.

"Need a refill?" Robyn sticks her head in the control room with a smirk. She's holding out a bottle of water in her hand that's dripping with condensation. A cooler is sitting on a wagon behind her, just outside of the control room.

I look back out at the guests filling the cabins of the ride so I don't have to say anything to her. I want to stay mad at her to drive home the point that I didn't like the way she acted on our date.

"Are you ignoring me?" she asks.

"No."

"Oh, my mistake. I guess it was the lack of response and sudden loss of eye contact that had me confused," she jokes.

I turn back to her and say, "Doesn't feel good to be ignored, does it?"

She makes a face. "Yeah, I guess I deserve that. Look, I just wanted to talk to you so I could apologize for what happened. It wasn't fair to you and I'm definitely not embarrassed of you. I guess I was just afraid that Peggy would get the wrong impression—or rather, the *right* impression—and use that as ammunition for the next time she's mad at me or something."

Down by the waiting line, Bailey gives me the thumbs up that all the cabins are filled and the doors locked, so I start the ride.

"I wish you would say something," Robyn says.

I sigh. "So what are you saying?"

"Well, if the offer is still on the table, I'd love to see you again. I miss talking to you."

Despite my best efforts, I grin.

"But..."

I glance at her out of the corner of my eye, making sure that my attention stays on the ride. "But what?"

"Things should be a little different. I'd prefer to keep whatever happens between us, well, *between us*. Nobody here should know."

I feel a bead of sweat roll down my face. "That's probably a good idea."

It's been several days since the disastrous date and I still haven't told anyone. Not even Max, who I've been spending more time with now that he lives with me. I told myself that I haven't mentioned her because I don't even want to think about her, but now I see that it was so I could protect whatever potential relationship that might come someday. Wishful thinking, I suppose, but I'm glad I kept my mouth shut.

"So…are you going to look at me, then?" she asks.

"Can't." A smile cracks my hard look, but it's okay. I'm glad for it.

"Why not?" There's a lightness to her voice too.

"I'm working. My boss would fire me if I killed someone."

"Uh, that's just the *tiniest* understatement."

I chuckle, still keeping my eyes on the ride. "It'd get publicity, though, right?"

She laughs. "That's so bad."

"You think it's funny. Actually, it was *your* joke."

"Well, how's this: I could use some help closing tonight. Peggy's been a big help all day with the water and I don't want to jinx it by asking her to stay."

"I'll help." I feel a burning sensation in the pit of my stomach that has nothing to do with the overbearing heat. It only makes me sweat more.

"Thanks." She looks out to the rest of the park and then back at me. "Do you want to come to my place for dinner tonight? As a sort of, uh, date do-over."

"What are you making?" I try to conceal my excitement.

"Oh, I don't know."

"Then I don't know if I'll come," I joke.

"What do you want?"

I grin. "I don't know."

She laughs. "You're impossible. Think about it and let me know. I need to get back to work. See you tonight."

"Can't wait."

She smiles at me as she walks over to the next ride to give a bottle of water to Mackenzie at the ladybug ride.

After Robyn hands Mackenzie her water, she kneels down beside a group of kids next in line. Soon the kids are giggling and jumping up and down with excitement. She really does love working with them.

§ § §

THE REST OF the day seems to drag now that I have something to look forward to. I wonder how I'll explain my absence tonight to Max, but I could just tell him that I have plans. Let him connect the dots on his own. As long as he doesn't figure it out completely.

Robyn doesn't mention anything about our date while she's closing the Pier's finances for the day, so I don't say anything either. Still, the anticipation for tonight and the fact that things are better between us is eating at me.

We chit chat on the way home, mostly about work. I try to steal glimpses of her eyes in the sun, but she's wearing her sunglasses. It isn't until we get to her front door that she asks me if I've decided what I want for dinner.

"Honestly, I haven't," I tell her. "Too nervous."

"Nervous?" She smiles. "I didn't think you got nervous."

"I can't help it."

"You're sweet. Come on inside and let's look at our options for food."

Her house is small. We step right into a large room that serves as the kitchen, dining room, and living room all in one. The wall directly across from us is filled almost floor-to-ceiling in windows that must bring in a lot of light each morning.

She motions to the door behind the stairs. "There's a half bath here and a full bathroom upstairs." She drops her bag on a barstool at the kitchen island.

"This is a nice place." I look around. The ceilings are tall and everything's painted white, which makes it look bigger. Large paintings hang below the staircase banister, mostly landscapes. "These are really nice."

"Thanks." She opens the large refrigerator fitted between two white cabinets. She grabs some vegetables and sets them on the black countertop. "This used to be a rental, but my dad bought it and renovated it."

"He did an awesome job."

"Yeah." She turns back to me. "So, I guess I actually don't have much."

"Who invites someone to their house for dinner without any food?" I laugh.

"Me, apparently. Anyway, I could make us some salads and grill up some chicken to add with it if you want. You're not, like, vegan or anything are you?"

"No," I say with a smirk.

"Good." She pulls everything out to start fixing dinner and I allow myself to wander a little bit.

I check out her backyard through the windows at the back of the house. It's all fenced in and there's a deck the width of the house just outside the French doors. The small shed in the corner of the yard is painted blue with white trim, the same colors as the house. A hammock hangs between the corner of it and a nearby tree. It provides additional seating for the small gas fire pit in the other corner of the yard.

"Small yard," I say. "It's really nice, though."

"Yeah, but it's just the right size for me. I'm not usually home, anyway."

"Even in the winter?"

"Especially in the winter."

I come over and take a seat at the small island. "Are you only here seasonally?"

"No, but I spend most of my time outside, regardless of the weather." She motions to the wall of windows. "Notice how my house is *basically* outside. Usually, I have those doors wide open to let the fresh air in."

"What do you do for a job in the off season?"

"I'm an artist. Painting, mostly."

"Really?" I wouldn't have pegged her as a painter with how strict everyone at work says she is. Artists tend to be more like free spirits. Then again, it's probably just her creative outlet.

Robyn chuckles and cuts up pieces of chicken. "Don't sound so surprised." She motions to the artwork on the wall. "You see that one of the sunrise? I did that. I was supposed to sell it, but I liked it too much."

I turn to look. "Wow. It's incredible."

"It better be for the hours I spend outside freezing my butt off when it's cold!"

"Now, don't get the wrong impression, but I've always had this vision that painters are…"

"Sloppy?"

"Yeah," I say with a chuckle.

She points upstairs. "Don't go in the spare bedroom, then."

I wonder if I'll ever get to go upstairs, but I keep that to myself. One thing at a time, Jaden. Things are already moving faster than I expected.

"Why do you work at the Pier if you're a painter?" I ask. "Isn't that more rewarding than yelling at Max?"

She laughs. "Yeah, it definitely is. But the Pier offers a steady income I can't count on with painting. Not to mention the change of pace to keep my creative mind active. And I love working with the kids."

"Too bad the sunsets aren't over the ocean here. I'm sure that would be really inspiring."

"The sunsets are still gorgeous."

I nod in agreement.

Within a few minutes she joins me at the island with two bowls of salad.

"So, don't think of this as another interview, but why don't you tell me more about yourself," she says. "Personally."

"What do you want to know?"

"Well, where did you go to college?"

"The Art Institute in Charleston."

Her jaw drops. "Are you for real?"

I shrug it off. "Yeah, but I'm not sure what I'm going to do with it."

"What was your concentration?"

"Photography, but I don't think there's any money in it."

"Well, not if you suck!" She giggles and adds, "I'm guessing you don't if you could get in there. Do you have some of your photos on your phone or a website or something? I'd love to see."

"They're not any good." I stab at my food with the fork.

"Let me see," she pushes.

I try to play it off like it's a bother, but really, I'm just glad that someone who isn't a professor is taking an interest in my photography. And it'd be nice to impress Robyn, too.

I pull out my phone and find the album with some of my shots. Several black and whites of family, a lot of the sunsets or clouds, and a few of the Ferris wheel I snapped while I was working.

She flips through them. "These are fantastic. You've got a great eye."

"Thanks."

She hands me back my phone. "No, I mean it. You really should try to pursue it. Build a portfolio. Maybe try to put together a studio of sorts. It'll be mostly portraits like wedding photos, senior pictures, that kind of stuff, but you could definitely sell your other stuff too if you have the right connections."

"Let me guess, *you're* the right connection?"

She shrugs with a smirk. "I could be one of them."

We finish eating and move out to the fire pit. Robyn lights it and then lies back in the hammock while I take a seat on one of the chairs on the other side of the fire.

"Aren't you going to come here?" she asks.

"Is there room for two?"

"We can make room."

I don't know why I'm nervous. I know Robyn. I'm the one who asked her out. But those few steps between the chair and the hammock are some of the most nerve-wracking of my life.

It takes a few awkward minutes, but we finally both get comfortable on the hammock. We lay side-by-side, looking up at the growing number of stars in the sky. There seem to be more here than North Beach. Less lights to drown them out.

She lays her head on my chest. "I can hear your heartbeat."

"Yeah?"

"Yeah. It's nice."

"Mm-hmm." I have my arm propped up behind her to push us off the shed so we keep swinging.

"See, this date is much better than our first." She turns to look me in the eyes.

"You say that like it's over." I push all of my nerves away and lean down to kiss her. It's just a quick one because the angle is awkward, but it's nice.

"That's it?" she asks. "I was expecting more."

I lean my head back and close my eyes as I laugh. "Well,

that's one way to kill a man's ego."

She chuckles. "No, I meant I wanted more."

I look back at her. "You do?"

"Yeah." She moves closer, pushing me back against the fabric of the hammock and kisses me with more passion than I ever expected her to. The burning sensation in my stomach comes back and seems to explode and spread throughout my body. It's as if this is all a dream.

Her hands find mine and our fingers intertwine. We kiss like that for a long while. I don't complain. I could stay like this forever.

She moves her one leg on the other side of me, as if she's going to straddle me, but when she shifts her weight, the hammock tips and we fall to the grass, both of us laughing as we try to untangle ourselves.

"Well, that wasn't quite what I was going for," she says.

I help her up. "Yeah, it was certainly a wake-up call."

She looks at me and slides her hands in her pockets. "Speaking of wake-up calls, you have an early one tomorrow. I guess you should probably get going."

"You're not working?"

She shakes her head. "It's my day off because I have to work the Fourth."

I forgot that the Fourth of July is in two days. I wonder how busy the Pier's going to be. North Beach is usually mobbed.

"What do you say tomorrow we do this at my place?" I ask. "Not—not this." I point to the hammock. "I mean, not unless you want to. I meant dinner. My roommate's usually gone on Thursdays."

She cringes. "Your place? I don't know."

I suck in my bottom lip to try to hide my disappointment. "Or we could just stick to your place." I just want to see her again.

She grins. "Yeah, that'd be nice."

"Good. I'll see you after work, then."

"Sounds like a plan."

I lean down and give her a quick kiss goodbye, although I know we both want more. Trouble is, we'd be here all night if we only did what we wanted. That thought alone will make for a long day tomorrow in anticipation for our next date.

Chapter Seven:

Robyn

I nibble on my turkey sandwich at the Nine while Adrian and Tyler work behind the bar. Tyler's washing glasses and Adrian's standing on a stool writing the drink specials on the chalkboard display.

"So what's been new with you?" Adrian asks over his shoulder. He looks down at a notepad before writing the next special on the board.

"Just working at the Pier," I say.

Tyler looks up. "Any new employees?"

I set what's left of my sandwich down and wipe my mouth. "Three, yeah. They're not bad."

"You mean they're not completely incompetent?" he asks.

I cringe. "Yeah, I guess I am pretty critical of the newbies."

"Try everyone," Adrian adds.

I roll my eyes. "I'm not that bad."

"Everyone at the Pier seems to think so," Tyler says. His sister is Bailey, who is another one of the ride ops.

"They all hate me anyway."

Adrian turns around to face me with a smirk. "I'm sure there's *someone* there who doesn't hate you."

My eyes bug out. "What do you know?" If Adrian knows about me and Jaden, that might mean that someone at the Pier knows too, which could get back to the owners.

Tyler looks between us. "What? What's going on?"

"Robyn's got a man-friend," Adrian teases.

"Where did you hear that?" I demand.

He laughs and gets down from the barstool. "Okay, don't freak out. It's not that big of a deal. Jessie called to ask about providing beverages for her party tomorrow—which I can't because the liquor license is restricted to this building—but she mentioned that you had a date with someone from the Pier."

"Oh." My cheeks go red and I slink back in my seat. Jessie, that makes sense.

Tyler looks over at me with a smile. "Oh? That's all we get? Who is this mystery man?"

I suppose it's probably a good sign that Tyler doesn't know about Jaden. That would mean he probably heard it from Bailey, which would mean that most of my employees know. Tyler's oblivious so my secret's still safe.

"One of her employees," Adrian tells him. "Based off a preliminary Facebook search, I found that he's single, a graduate of the Art Institute of Charleston, and really cute."

"You found all that from just his first name?"

"It's not like his name is Bob. There are only so many Jadens who work at the Pier. Actually, he's the only one."

"Oh, his name is Jaden?" Tyler cuts the water and grabs a towel to dry his hands.

"You've gotta give us something, otherwise we'll have to ask around for more details," Adrian says.

I groan. He's right. That would only raise suspicions that

Jaden and I are together. Well, confirm them.

"Last night was only our second date and it's still very new. If you ruin this I'm going to kill you."

Adrian puts up his hands in surrender. "I don't have any intentions of ruining it for you. I just want to know the details of what's happening in one of my best friend's love life."

"Jessie's? Is she still with Mason?" My lame attempt at changing the subject.

"We're talking about you," Tyler pushes.

I pick up my sandwich again to kill time while I think of another way to divert the conversation.

Adrian looks at his watch and then crosses his arms. "We don't open for another few hours, so we have time. If you want any more pre-opening food, you better spill."

"Okay, here it is: we went on a date because he kept helping me out at work."

"Bribery?" Tyler asks. "That seems like it's crossing a line."

"It doesn't take much for you, does it?" Adrian moves to the sink to wash the chalk off his hands.

"It's not like that," I say. "He asked me out. I like talking to him, so I said yes. But then when we were having ice cream—"

"*That* was your date? Robyn…" Adrian clucks his tongue and shakes his head.

"It was really hot that day!"

"I'm sure *somebody* was burning up," he mutters, drying his hands in a hand towel.

I ignore him and continue. "Anyway, I saw Peggy while we were out. She didn't see us, but I hid anyway. Jaden was mad. Thought I was embarrassed to be seen with him."

"Are you?" Tyler asks.

"No! I was just afraid that we would both lose our jobs if Peggy told the owners and that it'd look…well, *you know*." I wait for their reactions, but they don't say anything. "The rest of the workers already hate me. This would be just another reason."

"Sounds like you're overthinking this just a tiny bit," Adrian says.

"Maybe. Anyway, I apologized to Jaden and had him over for dinner last night—"

"Oooo," Adrian says as if he was hurt.

"What?"

"Your cooking could use some work."

"They were salads," I say.

He raises his eyebrows. "That's…romantic."

Tyler smacks him. "Ignore him. What did Jaden think?"

I shrug. "He seemed to like it. Anyway, afterwards we went out to the hammock and, well…" My cheeks flair up again.

Adrian giggles. "That's my girl!"

"Nothing happened! Well, not *that*."

Tyler smiles. "So you had a good time?"

"Yeah, and I really like him but…"

"What?" Tyler asks.

"I don't know." I shrug. "I'm his boss. That's crossing a line. And he's younger than me—"

"Age gaps are *not* that big of a deal," Adrian says quickly.

Tyler glares at him. I feel like I'm missing something, but I decide it's better not to push.

"Okay, so the age thing isn't really what's bothering me. I mean, it's only five years, but I guess I just have this feeling that it's…wrong."

Tyler shakes his head. "It's not wrong if you're happy."

"I agree." Adrian looks at him sternly when he says it.

"What's going on with you two?" I ask.

They turn away from each other.

"Nothing," Tyler says.

"Okay, then."

Adrian leans on the counter and takes my hands in his. "Do you like him?"

"I do."

"Then don't worry about the rest."

"Jessie thinks we might be better off waiting until the summer's over. When he's not my employee anymore. He'll probably move back to North Beach, though."

"The summer will only last so long," Tyler says. "Don't put off something that could be really great. Take advantage of it now."

"Yeah, you're right," I concede.

"When's your next date?" he asks.

"Tonight. But I also kind of want to spend tomorrow with him too, since it's the Fourth," I say. "The fireworks, the stars, lying in the grass. It seems romantic."

"Aw, it does!" Adrian says.

"What about Jessie's party?" Tyler asks. "We have to work tomorrow, so we can't go. One of us should probably be there to support her."

I make a face. "Oh yeah. I forgot. I also have to work."

"But you'll be done by time the fireworks start," Adrian says.

I sigh. "Yeah, I guess."

"Jessie's been kind of MIA since she's been with this new guy," Tyler says. "What's going on with that?"

"Are they still together? What happened after she bitch-slapped him here?" Adrian asks me.

"They argued a bit on the street—stuff with her ex, mostly," I explain.

The guys both nod in acknowledgement.

"Then we went back to her place and when I finally got her to calm down, I convinced her to try to talk to him to hear him out," I continue. "I don't know if she has, though. I haven't texted her. I probably should."

"Especially if you're going to ditch her tomorrow," Tyler adds.

"Yeah." I look at the time and see that I've been here too long already. "I should probably get going. There are some errands I want to run on my way home, plus I want to get something done on that landscape I've been working on. Besides, you guys probably have to get ready to open. Thanks for listening—even if you did drag it out of me."

Adrian smiles. "That's what we do."

§ § §

JADEN AND I are laying side-by-side in my backyard on a blanket I usually take to the beach if I ever get a moment to go. I've pulled out an assortment of snacks, but they mostly go untouched. We're waiting for the Fourth of July fireworks to start. They shoot them off from the beach, but I can usually see them pretty well in the sky from here. Perks of living in a small town.

It's still dusk, but any lingering sun from the day is quickly fading, making way for the beautiful night stars.

I hope Jessie's not mad at me. I texted her earlier today to tell her I couldn't make it to her party, which isn't entirely true. I probably should've at least stopped by on my way home from work and introduced her to Jaden. It just seemed too fast. We haven't been on that many dates. Instead, I avoided the Manor altogether, too excited to get the date started.

"The stars are starting to come out," Jaden says.

"Yeah. This is a pretty good spot to see them because there isn't a lot of light pollution from town."

"My dad used to drive me and my brothers out to a random field to watch them," he says. "We'd lie in the back of his truck and just stare for hours. Well, it seemed that way."

"That's nice. We used to just watch them from here."

"Your whole family lived in this tiny house?" he asks.

"It was just me and my parents," I say. "We stayed at the Manor when we came here the first time. That's how I met my friend Jessie."

"Who's that?"

"She owns the Manor by the beach."

"That big fancy building on the corner?"

I nod. "That's the one. Anyway, after my parents split up, my dad bought this house because he loved it here as much as I did. When I got the job at the Pier, I moved down here with him."

It's quiet for a while. The crickets chirp and a bird flies above us, but my mind is elsewhere.

"Your dad's not around anymore, is he?" Jaden asks softly.

I shake my head and feel the tears start to run down my face. "No. He was a smoker and one day he just dropped. I rushed him to the hospital, but that's all the way in North Beach. By then his lung had collapsed. He was at the hospital for a few weeks, but he didn't make it. It was all so fast."

I feel Jaden's hand grasp mine by my side.

"Robyn, I'm so sorry."

I wipe at my eyes and force myself to smile. "Sorry, I didn't mean to ruin the mood."

"Nonsense. I want to learn more about you."

I look over at him. "You're incredible."

He smiles. "I try."

I squeeze his hand back. "Thanks for listening."

"Anytime."

We're quiet again, but I'm perfectly content, even in the rush of memories of my dad.

"How did you get into painting?" he asks softly.

"I've always been painting. Ever since my parents first had me do that handprint turkey for Thanksgiving."

"Oh wow, so you started off an expert."

I laugh. "I was a prodigy, really. But no, as I got older—and better—I had moved to Montana Beach and would set up my stuff to paint different scenes. The buildings on First Street, our house, the sunrises. Those were Dad's favorites."

"I bet. The few I've seen are beautiful."

"Thanks." I look back to the sky. I wonder if we're going to be able to see anymore stars tonight or if the smoke from the fireworks will linger too much and obscure them.

"Tell me more about your dad," Jaden says.

"Well…he was so creative. Always loved to hear someone's story—especially from kids. He never thought they got enough time and attention to express themselves. He loved the sun, spent so much time outside. It's probably how he picked up smoking. Everyone smoked when he was younger and when he just wanted to be outside, it gave him something to do."

"What was your favorite thing about him?"

I consider this for a moment. "He was just so…genuine. He was real. Every time he said something, you knew he believed it with his whole heart, you know?"

"Sounds like a lot of him rubbed off on you."

I turn back to him and stare right into his big brown eyes. Before I know it, I'm leaning into him, just like I was last night and the night before, kissing him like I'll never see him again.

I hear the fireworks go off in the sky—can even see the colorful lights flashing through my eyelids—but I don't pay it any attention. I'm too preoccupied by the man lying beneath me. He's beautiful inside and out.

We stay tangled together for a long time—long after the fireworks have ended. This time, he's the one to break it off.

He sits up on his elbows. "As nice as this is, I should probably get going."

"What's the rush?" I can't even believe the words coming out of my mouth.

"It's getting late and…" He trails off.

I get to my feet and offer my hands to help him up. "Come on. We can get more comfortable upstairs."

"Wait, are you sure?" he asks, getting to his feet. "We've only been on a few dates. I don't mind waiting."

I kiss him once more to silence him. "Shh. I'm sure. This is what I want."

It doesn't matter how many dates we've been on. When you know, you know. While it's true that this is all happening so fast, a part of me is wondering why I ever questioned my feelings for Jaden to begin with.

Chapter Eight:

JADEN

"Oh wow, you've been busy." I sort through her collection of paintings in her art studio.

Robyn fusses with the clothes overflowing from the closet, but I pretend not to notice. She lives here, so I'd expect to see this place *lived in*.

"Yeah," she says, disappearing into her bedroom and returning shortly after. "It's what I do. Paint and see how many of them I can sell."

"I would think these would all have sold. They're incredible." They're all basically landscapes, several of the different stages of the sunrise over the ocean. One in particular is the sunset over the rest of the town. She must've gotten a pretty tall vantage point for that. Maybe at Montana Manor.

My favorites are the paintings of First Street. One in particular stands out to me. Instead of the half-empty storefronts that line the street now, Robyn paints what I can only imagine is her idea of the potential the street has. In her paintings, First Street is easily recognizable with its landmark buildings, but it's always filled with loads of people.

The longer I stare at it the more I see. The details of the buildings, the woman being pulled by her dog, a couple walking hand-in-hand, a mother pushing a baby stroller.

"How much is this one?" I ask.

Robyn seems surprised. "You want to buy one of my paintings?"

"Yeah, I love it."

"So do I."

"Oh!" It strikes me that she probably has a personal connection to all of these paintings. "Is this one not for sale?"

"No, nothing like that. It's just—it's one of my favorites. But I can't let you buy it. Just take it."

I shake my head. "No, this is how you make your money."

"You and I both know this isn't my only way of making money," she says. "It's fine, really. Just take it."

I look down at the painting again and then back to her. "No, you can definitely make a lot of money off of this one." I set it back down.

"So you're not even going to take anything?"

I smirk. "Here's an idea: if you really want me to have one of your paintings, why don't you paint me?"

She narrows her eyes. "You want me to *paint* you? Like a portrait?"

"Yeah."

"And you're going to hang a painting of yourself in your house?" She chuckles.

I shrug. "I'll probably give it to my mom, but I'd be sure to tell her where I got it from."

"Jaden, I don't know..."

"I'm not talking about a nude painting—"

"*That* would be a weird gift for your mother."

I laugh. "Just…a regular portrait. See if you can capture the real me."

"You don't think I can?"

I hook an eyebrow with a grin. "Will a challenge motivate you?"

"Maybe, but portraits aren't really my specialty. Landscapes are."

"But you can do it?"

"I could try."

I flash her a big smile, hoping it'll convince her.

"You really want this, don't you?" She steps over to the easel with a canvas half-covered in paint. There's a photo of a wave washing up on the beach beside it.

"That's why I challenged you to do it."

She sets the canvas aside carefully and pulls out a blank one from the closet.

"Challenge accepted, mister."

I bury my hands in my pockets. "So…how are we doing this? Am I just standing here like this or…?"

She puts a hand on her hip and thinks. "Hmm…if I'm going to capture the real you, I need to be able to paint you doing something you love."

"Are you talking about photography?"

"Yeah."

I hold out my hands palms up. "I don't have my camera with me."

"Hmm…" She looks around again. "Well, there's nothing saying we have to stay up here. Where's your favorite place here?"

My face breaks out into a huge smile and I start laughing.

She smiles and rubs her forehead. "A place that's *not* my bedroom."

"I guess out on the hammock."

"Then let's go."

I help her carry her things outside. The sun's setting, but we should have another hour or two of light. Robyn says that should be enough to get the basics down and she can do the rest from memory.

I lay back on the hammock and get comfortable, even closing my eyes once she gets started.

"That's it," she says. "Do you think you could hold that for a little while?"

I smile. "I'm not going anywhere."

"Good."

It's quiet as she gets to work. I reach up and start swinging, but stop when I remember she told me to sit still.

"No, that's fine," she says as if she read my thoughts. "If you're more comfortable that way. Just try to act natural. You can move a little, just as long as you keep the same general position."

I open my eyes and watch Robyn work. I'm not sure she's really paying attention to the fact that I'm watching her. She's so lost in the details of what she's seeing—what she's creating. Her brow furrows a little each time she looks up to make sure she's got the details right.

"Well, that's the best I can do for now," she says once the sun has set, casting the yard in darkness.

I get up to see what she's done. The image she's created blows me away. Even though it lacks certain details—still a work in progress, after all—it very clearly looks like me. Again, the longer I stare at it, the more I see. The more I recognize.

The fence, the sunlight, the hammock, *me.*

Somehow, with her creative prowess, Robyn's managed to almost capture a piece of me. As if part of my soul will forever live on with this painting. It's amazing.

"Do you like it?" she asks in a small voice.

I kiss her and hook my arm around her. "I love it."

§ § §

"JUST COMING IN for some extra water," I tell Robyn from the break room. I grab a bottle from the fridge and then peek into the office where she's sitting at the desk. "Oh, and this." I lean over and kiss her hard on the mouth.

She laughs and pushes me away. "Stop! Not in front of the camera!" She points above us. We've already determined that the security camera can't see us at this angle, but she's still paranoid.

"We'll be fine," I say. "But I should get back to work. I kind of left Max hanging at the end of the pier without a broom."

"Sounds like a bad joke," she says. "Now go! Before anyone notices you were in here too long!"

I give her another quick kiss before heading back out into the July heat. It's been a little over a week since Robyn and I first slept together and we've been nearly inseparable ever since. The only downside is that I don't live alone, which prevents her from coming to my place. And nobody at work knows. And we mostly only see each other at night.

Okay, lots of downsides. The good news is they're all temporary.

"What are you all smiley about?" Max says when I return to where we were working.

Robyn had me help clean today because it's the busiest part of the season, which means it's the messiest. The other cleaners needed the extra hand getting the Pier back in shape after the holiday rush.

"It's a nice day!" I hand Max the extra broom I brought back.

"No, it's more than that," he says. "You've been acting weird a lot lately."

"How have I been acting weird?" A big grin is spread across my face.

"Will you stop smiling like a weirdo!"

I try to act serious, but it doesn't work.

"Well, that's just creepier."

"Sorry you don't like my face," I counter.

"Not when you look like that. Geez." He turns and starts sweeping. "With a look like that, you'd think you were getting laid."

I don't say anything and start sweeping.

"Wait, *are* you seeing someone?"

"Why would you say that?" I don't meet his eyes.

"You are, aren't you?"

"What? No, I'm not." I turn my back to him.

He rolls his eyes. "You're the worst liar. Who is it? Is it Bailey? Mackenzie? Someone from town?"

I shake my head. "It's no one."

I'm actually kind of surprised that he didn't figure it out earlier. I mean, yesterday he nearly caught me and Robyn making out in the storage room. Luckily, we were able to play it off like she was showing me where we keep the extra hoses to wash the decking. Talk about a bad joke.

"Well, whoever she is, I hope I don't walk in on anything when I get back from my parents' tonight," he says.

My head snaps up. "You're not coming home tonight?"

"I told you this."

I vaguely remember him mentioning it this morning on the way in. "Right. Sorry, forgot."

Taking advantage of the momentary freedom from speculation, I move on to sweep the rest of the deck away from Max. He doesn't push me with anymore questions about the girl I'm seeing. Probably forgot already, to be honest. That's okay, because I'm too preoccupied thinking about tonight and how I'll have the house to myself, which means I can finally show it off to Robyn. However, she isn't as convinced when I suggest it to her at closing time.

"I don't know," she says as I finish counting out the day's money. "I wouldn't feel comfortable."

"In my house? I'm comfortable in your house." I set a stack of bills on the desk and punch the next hundred into the calculator.

"That's different."

I finish counting out the next hundred. "How so?"

"I don't have any roommates."

"But he's not going to be there," I say. Definitely not the best time to mention exactly who my roommate is. That would certainly make up her mind not to come.

"Jaden, our rule is no PDA outside of my house."

"That's only because your house is the only one that's guaranteed to be empty!" I set the rest of the bills onto the stack and add up my final numbers. I turn the calculator to her and say, "Here. Is this what you got?"

"Yeah, perfect." She turns back to the computer, apparently assuming our conversation is over.

After a moment, I say, "Robyn, look, I have a real nice place. I want to be able to share it with you. Your place is nice, but I'd like to switch it up every once in a while. Besides, if you stay, you don't necessarily have to go home."

She gives me a look. "You know I *really* wouldn't like it knowing your roommate's in the next room."

"But it's not like he'd come into my room."

"Jaden…" She waves her hand at me to try to silence me.

"Okay, maybe you don't spend the night. But you should still come over. I don't know what time he'll be back, but you can just hang out in my room until he goes to bed."

"And then sneak out? What is this, high school?"

"You're the one who wants to keep this a secret still. I'm just trying to follow your rules."

She considers this. "I suppose that's fair."

"Really?" My voice jumps an octave and I clear my throat to play it off.

She giggles. "Yeah, that's fine. But you better feed me."

I smile. "We can get take-out from the diner."

"Oh, how romantic." She stuffs the day's deposit into the bag and then tosses it in the safe.

"It's not that bad," I say. "A Montana Beach staple."

"Yeah, I guess you're right."

I call the diner and put in our order before we leave. Robyn's going home first so she can change. I head to the diner to pick up our food before meeting her at her house. I just hope this isn't a ploy to get us to stay at her place.

Luckily, she's already waiting on the front porch when I get there.

"You're ready."

She comes down the steps and meets me at the sidewalk. "You say that as if you're surprised."

"I am."

"Oh, gee thanks. It's not like I'm always early to work or anything."

I nod. "True. Sorry."

"So what's so special about this house that you want me to see it so bad?"

"It's mine."

She smiles and looks down at the sidewalk. "Right, sorry. I'm sure it'll be great—even if it's disgusting."

I laugh in surprise. "Give me a little more credit than that!"

"Hey, I'm just going off of what most guys are like."

"You should know by now that I'm not like most guys."

"That you aren't," she murmurs.

"I'm surprised you don't know what house it is, seeing how you're from Montana Beach."

She taps her chest. "Transplant. I don't know this town as

well as some people who've lived here their whole lives. Actually, I don't know if I've ever been on Cemetery Street. Between that creepy old motel and, you know, *the cemetery*, I try to avoid it."

We turn onto my street. "Isn't your dad buried in this cemetery?" I point up the street.

She shakes her head. "He was cremated and we spread his ashes in the ocean."

"Oh gotcha. That's nice, though."

"It's as close as he could get to that view of the sunrise each morning that he loved."

"Now he's a part of the sunrise."

"That's the way I like to think of it."

I point. "This is it."

She looks between me and the house in surprise. "Really?"

"What was I saying about giving me some credit?" I chuckle and lead her to the front door.

"I'm just—this house didn't used to look like that, did it?" She points to the fence by the old motel. "I mean, that eyesore can't be good for property values."

I shrug. "I don't know. The landlord said he recently renovated. Here, come on in."

She looks at the front porch as we step up. "You could use some lawn furniture."

"I'm just here for the summer." I pull out my keys and work the right one into the lock.

"Oh, right. I forgot."

"Well, maybe. Depends on how I like it."

She nods. "I remember now."

I lead her inside and watch as her mouth drops, just like Max's did when he first saw it. Only, it's a better look on Robyn.

"Jaden, *this* is your place? It's so nice! Honestly, I was expecting a tiny little dump, but this is—it looks like a family lives here. Well, minus the minimal living room furniture. The landlord couldn't have furnished it more?"

I shake my head with a smile. "Always a critic."

"Can't help it. It's in my blood."

"Come on, let's go eat on the back porch."

There isn't any furniture out here, either, but at least it's more private. Not that the unkempt lawn and green pool are a good view, but it's quiet. We sit with our feet hanging off the side of the deck and eat the subs we got from the diner. We watch the sunset until it disappears behind the neighboring houses.

"So you're really not sure if you're going to stay in Montana Beach?" she asks when she's finished eating. She leans against the support beam for the roof. Her sub wrapper is still laying flat beside her.

"It wasn't my intention to. Not unless I had a good reason to." I lick the last of the mayo off my thumb. All that's left of my sub. I wipe my hands with a napkin. "I was thinking a job would be that reason, but now I'm thinking otherwise."

"Like?"

I grin. She knows the answer already, but I don't want to say it. Too embarrassed, I guess. Besides, it's still early in our relationship. No sense in promising life-altering plans in case things don't turn out after the honeymoon phase is over.

"Anyway," I continue, "I'm just from North Beach, so it's not like it's that far anyway. Thirty or forty minutes, really."

"True, I just don't really like it there."

"But isn't it more about the people and less about the place?"

"Not when we're talking North Beach."

I laugh. "Okay, okay. You've got me there. But what about you? Are you going to stay in Montana Beach?"

"That's the plan."

"Even if the Pier closes?"

"That's not my only source of income."

"But it helps."

She shrugs. "Of course it does."

I look out into the yard. Somewhere, hidden in the grass, several crickets hide, filling the darkening sky with the sound of their chirps.

Robyn rubs her hands along her bare arms.

"Are you cold?" I ask her. "I can get you a blanket. Or we could go inside."

She hooks an eyebrow. "To the bedroom?"

I look down, embarrassed. "Not exactly what I meant, but I wouldn't turn it down."

It's quiet for a moment and I'm afraid my response was too presumptuous until I look up at her.

"Sure," she says.

"Really?"

"Isn't that what we usually do anyway?"

"But I don't want it to be *all* we do."

She smiles. "We work together, remember? And we talk. Not to mention, we're young, we're alone, and as long as your bedroom doesn't smell like a locker room, I'm content with spending the evening with you."

I smile, but inside I'm wondering when the last time was that I did my laundry. Or how full my tiny little garbage can is. Or if I made my bed this morning. Instead, I push all that away and stand to take her hand and lead her inside.

I lock the front door and turn the lights off, leading her to my room. I don't turn on the light because there aren't any curtains or anything over the large window looking onto the front porch. Plus, my room *could* be tidier. The darkness will hide some of it.

"It's quiet." Robyn wraps her arms around me.

"It's just us." I take her hand and we sway as if we were dancing, even without any music. After a few minutes, she kisses me, pulling me down onto the bed.

"Wait, the door." She points behind me.

I get up and close it. "Better?"

"Much. Come here."

Eagerly, I lie next to her on the bed and kiss her. I work my hand under her shirt and she grasps at my back, tugging at the fabric of my shirt until she pulls it off.

I'm about to do the same to her when I hear footsteps on the porch. Keys jingling. My heart nearly stops. I look through the window and see Max fumbling with his keys on the porch. I'm glad I didn't turn the lights on. Hopefully he hasn't seen us.

Moving forward to get a better view, I watch as he disappears inside. I collapse on the bed, breathing a sigh of relief for the moment.

I look over at Robyn. Her eyes are wide.

"*Max* is your roommate?"

Chapter Nine:

Robyn

I jump up and grab the shoes I kicked off at the foot of the bed. Luckily, I didn't leave them out by the front door. I sit on the edge of the bed and pull them on, a mixture of annoyance, worry, and anger bubbling in me.

Jaden pulls on his shirt and I glare at him. I want to yell at him for not telling me that he lives with Max—I never would've agreed to come if I had known that—but now's not the time. I just want to get out of here without being seen.

He leans in close to my ear and mutters, "I'm going to go out and distract him. You go out the window."

I nod and hide around the corner while Jaden leaves the room. Once he's gone, I press my ear against the door and listen for the best moment to escape.

"You're home early," Jaden says.

"Yeah, my folks wanted to turn in," Max replies.

"Are you just going to watch TV, then?"

"Is that okay?"

"That's fine, I just thought you were working tomorrow. I figured you'd probably turn in early." It's not hard to tell that Jaden's lying. I'm guessing that they don't typically have these types of conversations.

"Are you okay?" Max asks. "You're acting weird."

"I'm fine."

There's a pause. "Is there a girl here?"

Guess that's my cue to go. I rush to the window and try to slide it open, but it won't budge. Newer windows, too. I wonder if—ah, there it is, the lock. I unlatch it and slide the window up slowly, trying to keep from making any noise.

"Do you two want privacy?" Max snickers.

I pop out the screen, set it on the bed and carefully step out the window onto the front porch. I can't believe I'm doing this. I've never snuck out like this—well okay, I *have*, but I thought I was past this kind of stuff.

I hear Jaden say, "I'm going to bed," just as I jump down onto the grass. Keeping close to the fence with overgrown vines on it along the former motel, I rush to the sidewalk and around the corner until I'm out of sight. I break into a run and don't stop until I'm home.

I lock the door behind me and lean against it, slinking to the floor as I catch my breath. After a few minutes my phone dings. A text from Jaden.

Sorry! Good thing he didn't catch us in the middle of it!

I rest my head back against the door and smile. This evening hasn't turned out the way I thought it would, but I have to admit that it's certainly memorable. I smile and before I realize it, I'm laughing. I just snuck out like I was in high school again, running down the street as if someone was chasing me.

Another text from Jaden: *Really sorry :(Should've just listened to you.*

Don't worry about it, I write back. It's actually kind of funny now.

As long as you're not mad.

Did he say anything else?

Not really.

Good, I write. *See you tomorrow.*

§ § §

I WARM MY hands around my coffee at work the next morning. It rained a bit late last night and the sun hasn't quite warmed everything up yet. It doesn't help that the office AC runs on a timer. I don't want to turn it off because tomorrow will probably be a scorcher. Hell, even later today could be.

I had intended to work on Jaden's portrait some more this morning, but after last night, I knew I wouldn't be in the right headspace to paint him. Instead, I worked on the sunrise landscape in the spare room. It's getting there, little by little.

There's a soft knock on the door frame and I nearly jump until I see it's Jaden. "Hey," he says.

"Morning."

He takes a seat across from me. "So last night was, uh…"

I look down at my cup. "Yeah."

"Again, I'm really sorry about that. I never would've insisted you come over if I had known he'd be back that early."

I smile. "It's okay, you didn't know."

We're quiet for a few seconds and then I say, "So Max is your roommate?"

He drops his head and sighs. "Yeah."

"You should've told me."

"I know."

"I never would've come if I had known that he lived there too. Were you trying to trick me or something?"

"No!" he says quickly. "No, I just wanted to show you where I lived because…I don't know. I care about you and I wanted to show you another part of me."

That makes me smile, but I try to hide it. "You still should've told me."

"I know. And I'm sorry. I won't hide stuff from you again."

"Oh really? You're going to make that kind of promise this early?" I chuckle.

He smiles back at me. "I guess I am."

I grin, but don't add anything else.

"Max definitely suspects something, though," he says.

"Oh?" I take a sip of my coffee to hide my surprise.

"Not that it was you, just that there was *someone*. But then, he's been thinking that a lot lately."

I make a face. "I guess we have been kind of obvious."

"I wouldn't say obvious, just…not careful."

"Yeah, we should definitely change that. No more sneaking around. Not even when we're alone," I say. "From now on, any physical contact between us is off limits unless we're somewhere private."

"You mean your house," he clarifies.

I shrug. "That *is* the only place we haven't been caught."

"We haven't been caught anywhere!" he says playfully. "Last night was the closest we've come."

"You're forgetting about that time in the storage room."

"Oh yeah."

"Seriously, Jaden. If we both want to keep our jobs, we have to be more careful."

He nods. "Yes, ma'am."

I smirk. "What did I say about calling me that?"

He grins. "It seemed fitting."

"Anyway, you should probably get ready for work."

"Just one more thing."

"Yes?"

"Do you want to try again tonight?" he asks. "This time at

your place, of course."

I cringe. "Tonight?"

"What, did last night freak you out too much?" He looks nervous.

I shake my head. "No, it's not that. I have plans tonight."

"Oh."

"Yeah, you know how my friend Jessie runs the Manor?" I point in the general direction. "Anyway, she and her grandma are having a fundraiser tonight at the Nine and since I missed her Fourth of July party to be with you…"

"You want to be with her tonight," he finishes for me. "It's okay. I get it. You have friends who want to see you. I'll be fine."

I study him for a second. "Do you want to come?"

"Is that allowed?"

I shrug. "Yeah, I mean, it should be a larger crowd. People shouldn't really pay too much attention to us being together."

He gives me a look.

"Not like, *together* together, but talking outside of work," I clarify.

"You've put a lot of thought into this."

"One of us had to, otherwise I'd be crawling out of your bedroom window every night."

He groans. "I made one mistake!"

"I'm kidding." I laugh. "For real, though, you should get ready for work."

He smiles. "Okay. I'll see you tonight then."

"Can't wait."

§ § §

I TOLD JADEN to meet me at the Nine so it didn't look as obvious that we're together. I know I'm just being paranoid, but after last night I don't want to take any chances. Besides, I wanted time to go home and get ready. This is likely the biggest social event I'm going to this summer. Best not to look like I just strolled out of work.

I'm pleased to see the line to get in stretches a good way down First Street. That must mean that the Manor is making a lot of money tonight. I take my place in line and text Jaden to see if he's here.

Almost at the door. Come up here, he writes back.

I walk down the crowded street until I find him. "Hey, you look nice," I say.

He's wearing a white polo and dark jeans. I suppose it's nothing special, but it does look nice on him. It's a better look than the Pier uniform I usually see him in.

"Thanks," he says. "So do you."

I'm wearing jean shorts and a flowy yellow top.

"Have you ever been here?" I ask.

He shakes his head. "No, but I've heard it's good."

"It's the best. Two of my friends work here. Actually, one of them owns it."

"Oh wow, that's cool."

"Yeah, sometimes I can sneak in before they open and have lunch," I say.

"That's cool. So what's the deal with this fundraiser?" he asks.

"Oh, it's for Montana Manor. It's not doing so hot financially—a byproduct of the whole town not doing so hot—and some developer wants to tear it down. Jessie's hoping the fundraiser will help save it. There's going to be music and drinks and a basket raffle and stuff. I donated a couple season tickets to the Pier for it. I hope it helps."

"Well, the party looks like it's a success."

I scan up and down the street at the line of people. They're all different ages, but most of them are actually younger. Well, my age. Not that that's old, but it's not exactly teenaged.

“Yeah, but I wonder how many of these people are here for the fundraiser or just here for a drink,” I tell him.

“Either way, it’ll help her out, won’t it?”

“It should. This bar is really cool because even though it’s in the basement, the back half of it opens right up to the beach, so it doesn’t feel like a basement, you know?”

“That’s what I heard from some of the people at work,” he says.

I can tell he’s trying very hard to be cordial, to not be flirty with me and draw attention. The crowd makes it easier not to be as playful with him. I know there are eyes on us.

We’re almost to the door when I hear a familiar voice from across the street. My heart nearly stops when I see Max coming toward us.

“So *this* is where you were rushing off to!” he says to Jaden. A big smirk spreads across his face when he spots me. “And with Miss Boss, herself!”

“Max, it’s not what it looks like,” Jaden says quickly.

“Not what—oh, so *you* were the girl sneaking out last night,” he says loudly, pointing at me.

Jaden grabs his arm and leads him out of line and around the corner onto Ocean Boulevard, just out of sight of the crowd on First Street. I follow closely behind.

“Hey, easy man!” Max shouts at Jaden, shrugging out of his grasp.

“Max, please keep your voice down,” I say.

“What? You don’t want everyone to know YOU’RE SCREW—”

Jaden covers his mouth with his hand. “I *swear…*”

“Jaden, don’t,” I warn.

Slowly, he pulls his hand away.

“So how long has it been?” Max asks in a quieter voice.

Jaden and I look at each other and then both look away quickly.

"Not long," Jaden says.

"Just a few weeks," I add.

"A few weeks?" Max looks surprised. "Damn, I didn't think you could stand her that long."

"Don't be rude," Jaden says.

"I'll say what I want."

"That's enough!" I whisper-shout. "Can we act like grown adults for two seconds, please?"

Jaden and Max stare at each other, neither of them moving.

I turn back to Max. "Look, we kept it a secret because we just wanted to keep it between us for now. We didn't want anyone to get the wrong impression."

"That he only got the job because you're screwing him?" Max asks.

"Hey, I do more in a single day than you've done—"

I squeeze Jaden's arm to silence him. When he's quiet, I turn back to Max.

"I hired him before we ever did anything together. You have to believe that."

"Why should I?"

"Because it's the truth!" My cheeks burn and I drop my voice. "Look, I know you don't owe us anything, but I'm asking you to please keep this quiet. Can you do that for us? Please?"

Chapter Ten:

JADEN

Max considers Robyn's proposal for a minute. It seems to take longer than a minute because a lot weighs on his response. He could—and would—make a huge deal about me and Robyn. At that point, the best I could do is quit so that Robyn might be able to keep her job. But if I want to stay in Montana Beach, I need this job.

Finally, Max smiles and says, "Okay. I'll keep it quiet."

Robyn and I both breathe a sigh of relief. Bullet dodged. For now, at least.

"On two conditions," he adds.

I glare at him. That feeling of relief didn't last long.

"What is it?" Robyn asks.

"I'll keep your secret if you let me have Fridays *and* Saturdays off."

"Those are our busiest days," she says.

"And second, you need to stop being so hard on me at work," he continues. "No more calling me out for being late, no more yelling at me to clean up, none of it."

"That's your job, you moron," I snarl.

He puts up his hands in surrender. "Those are my stipulations. I'm not saying I'm not going to do my job, but I'll get to it when I can."

How lazy can one person be?

"So you want to do nothing but still get paid for it?" I ask. "That's completely unreasonable! You can't expect us to—"

"Okay," Robyn says over me.

"Okay?" Max and I ask in unison.

She nods. "Fine, whatever you want. As long as you keep it quiet."

"Robyn, you can't be serious." Neither one of them pay attention to me.

Max holds out his hand and Robyn shakes it.

"Pleasure doing business with you, boss," he says.

I watch as Max walks off triumphantly and wait until he's out of earshot to say anything. When I turn to question Robyn further, I can see the panic in her eyes. She looks like she's on the verge of tears. I suck in a deep breath and push my anger away. She doesn't need it right now.

"Do you want to just go home?" I ask.

She shakes her head. "No, we need to go in. I've already bailed on Jessie once. I need to make an appearance here, even just for a little bit."

I nod. "Okay."

We get back in line and don't say anything until we're inside. I follow Robyn as she meanders to the bar. The bartender is a thin man with his black hair slicked back. He looks to be about our age. Maybe a little older than me. Robyn waves him over as we find two seats in the corner.

"I wanted to introduce you to someone," she says. "This is Jaden." She points to the man, "This is Adrian. He's my friend who owns the bar."

I shake his hand. "This is an awesome place. I've never been in here before."

Looking around, I really take in the space. Old photos of the buildings along First Street hang on the exposed brick wall we're tucked next to. Behind the bar, several small square chalk boards list the drink specials with unique names like Captain's 'Cap, Beach Bracer, and Seaside Swig.

"Well, welcome! And thank you!" He puts his hands on his hips and looks around. "Yeah, this place took a lot of hard work—still does—but I think it's worth it." He looks over at Robyn. "What's the matter? You seem upset."

She forces a smile. "No, I'm fine."

He lifts his eyebrows and glances at me.

She plays with the stack of coasters in front of her for a few seconds before responding. "I think I might get fired."

It's hard to tell with the music, but I swear I hear her voice crack. Either way, I rub her back to try to comfort her.

Adrian looks concerned. "What? Why? What's going on?"

"Because of me and him." She motions to me. "One of my other employees just saw us and threatened to tell everyone."

"Oh. But that doesn't necessarily mean you'll get fired."

Robyn looks at him through her eyebrows. "He'll probably tell the owners, too."

"Oh. Do you think he's going to?"

She shrugs. "He promised he wouldn't, but I wouldn't put it past him."

"Is it that screw-up guy you're always complaining about?"

She doesn't answer, so he looks at me. I nod.

He leans on the bar and reaches for Robyn's hands. "Honey, look, if he's really that bad of an employee, the people who matter are not going to believe him. And even *if* the owners do come check on you, you'll be your usual badass self at work and they'll realize how lucky they are to have you."

"Maybe."

"Just be more careful to keep your personal business separate when you're at work."

She doesn't say anything or even look at him, still busying herself with the coasters.

One of the other waitresses calls for Adrian. He gives her a nod and then turns back to Robyn. "Hang in there. It's not the end of the world." He looks up at me. "Nice to meet you. Order a drink!"

When he's gone, I look down at Robyn. She glares up at me.

"What?" There's an edge to her voice.

"Nothing."

She shakes her head. "I know it's not nothing. What are you thinking?"

I consider it for a moment. I was going to wait longer before I brought it up. When we were alone. When she was feeling a little better about what just happened. But she's asking me now and I'd rather not build any sort of resentment between us.

"I'm just surprised that you gave in to Max's demands so quickly," I finally say.

"What was I supposed to do?"

I shrug. "I don't know, fire him? Tell him to go to hell? Ignore him?"

She tries to get up, but she's blocked in. "Jaden, I could get *fired*. You could, too. The whole Pier could shut down in a few years if the right person isn't managing it."

"Maybe, but like Adrian just said, it's not the end of the world. We'll get through it."

She looks up at me. "And if you don't have a job, what's going to keep you here? Sure, North Beach isn't that far, but it's not that close, either. Why would you continue a relationship with someone you have to make an effort to see?"

I drop my shoulders and look at her. "Is that really what's bothering you?"

She shrugs and looks away. "I just liked it when our relationship was just ours. Nobody else knew about it. That didn't last long enough."

I lean forward until our foreheads touch. "What's going to keep me here is you because I care a lot about you. Even if we don't work together it doesn't mean we can't be together." I kiss her softly. "Come on, let's get this off your mind for a little bit."

She takes my hand and leads me through the crowd out onto the beach. Several people sit around a large roaring fire. In the distance, the waves continue to wash onto the shore.

"Ah! You made it!" a blonde girl exclaims. She pulls herself out of the embrace of a blond man and runs to hug Robyn.

"Wouldn't miss it," Robyn says with what I can tell is forced enthusiasm. "This is a great turnout! You guys must be making a killing."

The blonde nods. "We are, yeah. Actually, the mayor just told off the developer, so it looks like the Manor is saved!" She motions over to the man she was just laying with. "Oh, and you remember Mason, right?"

Robyn smiles. "Oh sure, hi!" She gestures to me. "And this is Jaden. Jessie's the one from Montana Manor I told you about," she tells me.

I reach over and shake their hands. "Nice to meet you both."

Jessie's smile hasn't left her face since we first came out here. But then, I bet I'd be smiling too if my livelihood was just saved. "Oh, so I see you two have gotten back together!"

"Back together?" I ask. "When did we break up?"

Robyn rolls her eyes. "Oh, I saw her right after our first date."

"Ooo." I make a face. "Yeah, that was bad."

"You're the ones who work at the Pier, right?" Mason asks.

"Yeah, but I don't know for how much longer," Robyn says.

"Don't say that," I say.

Jessie's smile fades. "Why? What's going on?"

"I'm just not sure if the owners are going to like this." She waves between us.

"How are they going to know?" Jessie asks.

"They're not," I respond, but Robyn ignores me.

"One of my other employees might tell them."

"Robyn, what are you going to do?" Jessie looks worried, which I'm sure doesn't help with what Robyn's feeling.

"I don't know! I mean, I knew going into this that it probably wasn't the best idea because we'd have to keep it a secret. I just thought the secret would last a little longer. If people knew about us they wouldn't respect me anymore as a boss. Do you think I'm being dumb?"

I turn my attention to the fire. How could she think that?

"Are you from Montana Beach, too?" Mason asks while the girls continue to chat.

I shake my head. "No, North Beach. You?"

"I'm from New York, but my company is opening an office down here that I'm going to run, so I'll be moving soon."

I nod. "Nice."

"What do you do?"

"Just the Pier for now."

"Oh okay. I'm sure it's a fun job."

I give him a tight smile because I don't really feel like chit-chatting right now. Robyn's whole attitude is eating at me.

"Well, we should get going," Robyn says. "I just wanted to stop by because I missed your Fourth of July party."

Jessie waves it off. "Oh, don't even worry about it. It worked out okay." She gives Robyn a hug. "I'm so glad you made it! Thanks for coming!" She looks over at me. "It was so nice to meet you. I'm sure we'll be seeing a lot more of each other."

I force a smile. "Yeah, maybe." I shake Mason's hand one

more time before Robyn and I weave our way back through the crowd to the door.

We're quiet as we walk down First Street and onto Montana Boulevard.

"I need to talk to you about something," I say after several minutes of silence.

"Is it about Max again?" She sounds exasperated. It's obviously still on her mind, too. "I already told you, I had no other choice."

"Didn't you?"

"What does that mean?"

"You just seem so focused on the negative of what *could* happen that you were kind of a jerk to me."

She stops and looks at me with an exaggerated expression. "How am I being a jerk to you?"

"You make it seem like you don't actually want to be with me." I keep walking and she follows.

"If I didn't want to be with you, I would've just broken up with you instead of giving in to Max."

"Would you have?" I ask. "Or are you more concerned with people knowing you were ever with me at all?"

"What are you talking about?"

"You told Jessie that there's no way anyone would respect you if they knew about us. Why? Is it because I only work at the Pier? Is it because I'm from North Beach? Or is it just me in general? What is it about me that you *actually* like?"

She tugs at my arm to stop me. "Hey, there are a lot of things about you that I like. I just think that if people knew about our relationship they wouldn't like me as a boss anymore."

"Open your eyes, Robyn! Nobody likes you now!"

My words seem to physically hit her. I immediately want to take them back.

"As a boss, I mean."

She shakes her head. "No, you said what you said. Nobody likes me, I get it. Maybe *you're* the one ashamed of *me*. Is it because I'm the boss? Or is it because I supposedly have a stick up my ass and am always on everyone about doing their damn jobs!"

"Don't turn this around on me," I shout back, angry at her response. "I have done nothing but try to impress you. What have you done for me? Hide when people are looking? Give in to stupid demands to keep our relationship a secret? Write it off as one of your regrets?"

"You know what? Maybe there's just a simple solution here that we need to consider," she says. "If neither of us actually *like* each other, then what the hell are we even doing?"

"That's a good question."

She studies me. "I think I can walk home by myself, thanks."

I watch as she leaves. I debate whether to chase after her and apologize or let it go and make this whole ordeal go away.

Ultimately, I turn and take the long way back to my house. We both work at the Pier, so it's not like this will go away so easily. We'll see each other tomorrow. We'll probably talk after we've both calmed down.

I wonder, though, will the solution still be the same?

When I get home, Max is digging through the fridge in the kitchen.

"Did you have a nice date?"

"Shut up." I reach around him to grab a glass from the cupboard and fill it with water at the sink.

"What?" he snickers. "Are you seriously mad at me? Dude, you should've told me you were banging the boss!"

I glare at him. "Yes, I'm mad at you. Why did you have to be such a jackass to her?"

"Because she's always such a jackass to me! I'm just giving it back to her."

"You put everyone's jobs at risk."

Max rolls his eyes. "You're being so dramatic about this. I'm just having a little fun. If I can get weekends off in the process, why wouldn't I take advantage of it?"

"I shouldn't be surprised," I mutter as I walk to my bedroom. "You really are a horrible person inside and out."

"And don't you forget it!" Max calls after me with a chuckle.

Chapter Eleven:

Robyn

It takes all of my effort not to think about what happened at the bonfire or the walk home. For the first time all summer, I'm actually late to work this morning, just so I can avoid the possibility of seeing Jaden. I don't think he would come in early to chat, but after what we both said to each other and with the fate of our jobs resting in the hands of Max, it's better for us to just keep our distance.

Today's staff is waiting for me in the break room when I walk in. Peggy leans against the wall at the front of the room and scrolls through her phone. From the back, Jaden looks right at me when I walk in, but quickly looks down at his phone when our eyes meet. Max is laughing with some guys at the front of the room. Bailey and the rest of the staff are all engaged in private conversations.

Well, until I walk in. Almost everyone looks at me with confused looks when they see me with my bag slung over my shoulder and my coffee in my hand—it's very obvious that I'm just getting here, not out on the Pier cleaning or something.

I hastily toss my bag on the chair in the office and come back out to address the room, which has gone silent. For a moment, I debate whether I should say anything about my tardiness, but I don't.

"Morning," I start.

It's echoed back to me in unenthused voices.

"Uh, some goals for today should be to make sure to drink a lot of water—it's another hot one—and see if there's anything else we can do to go above and beyond for the guests," I say. "Let's get some ideas going. Anyone have any?"

Max raises his hand and I do my best not to react to it, but I can feel my shoulders tense up.

"Yeah, I have one," he starts.

"What is it, Max?" I sip my coffee and try to come off as bored.

"Why should we be the ones going above and beyond when you can't even show up to work on time?"

I sigh. He's got a point. I really should've gotten here earlier for no other reason than to give me time alone at work before I had to deal with him.

"Okay, you're right," I say. "Instead, let's say a goal is to make sure the Pier is spotless all day long. How's that sound? I'll even personally be out there sweeping today to make up for my late morning."

This seems to pacify some of the staff, but, of course, not Max.

He snickers. "I don't want to."

I meet his eyes and consider saying something snarky or even just writing him up, but I don't. Although he's been lazy, he's been good for most of the summer with the point system and I don't want to risk him blurting out that Jaden and I are—*were*—together.

I stare at him for a moment and then look away to the rest of the group. "Let's just have a good day, everyone. Okay?"

"Sounds shitty." He chuckles but the rest of the room seems to ignore him as they shuffle out the door. I'm grateful for it.

I take another big gulp of my coffee and step into the office to do some of the morning paperwork. The computer is already on, which is odd.

"What was that?" Peggy steps into the office and shuts the door behind her.

"That was the morning meeting." I turn to open the safe and look for the register drawers, but they're not in there. "What happened to—?"

"I already did them."

I'm surprised, but immediately wipe it from my face. "Oh, thanks."

"One of us had to do our job while you slept in," she says. "What's the deal? You seem off."

I click around on the computer, even though there isn't anything left to do. "I don't want to talk about it."

"You don't want to talk about letting one of your employees stand around with his hands in his pockets?" She looks out the window. "That's what he's doing right now."

I look up. "Who?"

"Max."

"Oh."

"That's it? You're giving up on him?"

I shrug. "He's never listened to me before."

"But you still kept on him."

"Peggy, I don't want to talk about it."

"So what do you want me to do about Max?"

"Jaden can pick up the slack."

She turns to open the door but stops and spins around again. "Is he the reason you were late?"

"Max?"

"No, Jaden."

My heart beats a little faster and I finish off my coffee to hide my panic. "Why would you say that?"

"You two have been joined at the hip all summer. All of a sudden today you show up late and neither of you have even looked at each other."

I glance up and see Peggy narrowing her eyes.

"Are you two—?"

"No!" I nearly shout, diverting my eyes back to the computer. "No, we're not—whatever it is you were going to say." My cheeks burn with embarrassment. Smooth, Robyn, real smooth.

I brace myself for the laugh or some other ridicule, but instead Peggy takes the seat across from the desk and waits for me to meet her eyes.

"Has it been all summer?" she asks in a quiet voice.

I nod.

"Okay." She pauses. "A few other people have noticed how close you two have gotten—specifically in the last few weeks. They've asked me about it, but I've been trying to kill those rumors."

"Thanks," I mutter.

"They still suspect," she adds.

I nod.

Of course they suspect. I haven't been acting like my usual self. I've been favoring Jaden. Talking to him before anyone else came in each morning, asking him to stay late to help me close, sneaking around to kiss him like we're teenagers who can't keep their hands off each other. Maybe what they say is true: love is blind. In all aspects. I couldn't see how obvious we were being.

My stomach begins to churn and I feel queasy from it all. It's not that I'm embarrassed about Jaden, I'm embarrassed about being so strict on the rules and then breaking them the moment it was convenient for me. I'm a hypocrite.

"Can I be alone for a minute?" I ask.

Peggy doesn't say anything, but she does leave the room.

I lean back against the chair and shut my eyes tight, willing myself not to cry, but my moment of solitude doesn't last long. To my utter annoyance, Max walks through the door with a snide grin on his face.

"What?" I ask with a little more of an edge than I intend.

"Easy. Is that the thanks I get for keeping your secret?"

I debate whether it's even still a secret anymore but let him talk.

"I need an advance on my paycheck."

"Next week is the pay week," I say.

"I know. Hence, me calling it an 'advance.'"

I look at him, fighting the urge to roll my eyes. "What do you need it for anyway?"

"I have things to do."

"Like?"

"Don't worry about it." He holds out his hand. "Now, are you going to pay up, or am I going to have to make an announcement?"

I think about the worst thing that could happen if the owners find out. I'd lose my job. Jaden would surely lose his, too. The owners might not want to be bothered finding a new manager for a business that doesn't bring in a lot of profit, so they might close the Pier, which would mean all of the other employees would lose their jobs too. Another staple in Montana Beach would disappear.

It all rests on this moment. I don't really have a choice.

"Fine," I say. "Just give me until the end of the day to shift some money around and I'll pay you based off the hours you worked in the last pay period. But you have to actually *work* those hours. It also means your next paycheck won't be until the following payday, got it?"

He shrugs with a smirk. "We'll see."

I bite my tongue to keep my words in until he's out of the room and then swear under my breath. We have the money, sure, but we can't keep giving him advances. Not to mention, I don't want to enable that kind of behavior. If we were ever audited, I'd be fired anyway.

Opening up the Pier's finances spreadsheets, I try to determine where I can momentarily pull money from to pay him off. My mind can't get off the fact that he's the worst employee on the payroll, though.

I rub my face in my hands and groan. I can't believe it's come to this. He knows how to do his job well, but he's so lazy and it's a battle every time I want him to do anything.

On the calendar, I count up the number of days it's been since he's been late. Twenty. I thought these last few weeks were an indication that this summer would be different for him. Guess not. The moment he saw an opportunity to take advantage, he took it. I just hate being sucked into that kind of behavior.

I pull out his file and look through it. There are three other employee termination forms that are filled out halfway. That means at three separate times I thought I was going to fire him but he turned it around.

I pull out a fresh one and consider actually going through with it now, but I can't. He would definitely call the owners then or start rumors about me and Jaden. In such a small town, word would spread quickly. And it wouldn't be just my name being dragged through the mud, but Jaden's too. He doesn't deserve that.

I sit back in the chair and chew on the end of my pen, weighing my other options. I half wonder if Jaden can try to convince Max to not say anything—or maybe he already tried—but I don't want to put the stress on Jaden. No matter where we stand with each other now, I care about him. A lot.

The trouble is, I know Max's demands will only continue. First, it was his ridiculous work schedule, now it's a pay advance—what will he ask for next? When will it end?

It won't.

There's a knock at the door and I blink away my tears, hoping it's not Max.

"Are you coming—" Peggy starts to say until she sees me. She shuts the door behind her. "What's the matter?"

I wave it off and reach for a tissue. "It's stupid."

"Is it about Jaden?"

"Sort of," I mutter.

"Did you guys have a fight?"

"No—well, yeah, but that's not—it's Max."

"Max?" She rubs her forehead. "Okay, I need you to back up here. How does Max fit into this?"

"He knows about us."

"Is that what this morning was about?" she asks. "I just thought he was being his normal self, but he seemed to be extra belligerent today."

"Yeah, because he's trying to blackmail me."

Peggy takes a seat on the corner of the desk. "What do you mean?"

"He just came in here and asked for an advance on his paycheck if I wanted him to keep it quiet."

"You're not thinking of paying him, are you?"

I shrug.

"Robyn, you can't be serious!"

"What am I supposed to do?" I shout. "I could get fired! So could Jaden! Maybe even this whole park would—"

"What? Close?" she asks with a disbelieving look. "Do you really think there's no one else in the world that could do this job as well as you?"

"Well, no," I say in a small voice.

"They'd find someone. The Pier would go on," she says. "And so would you. This isn't your only job. You have art too."

I look up at her. "How do you know about that?" I never usually mention my art because nobody asks about my life outside of the Pier.

"It's a small town, I read about you in the weekly paper. Not to mention, I've seen you lugging your art supplies down to the beach in the off-season."

I smile. Guess Peggy's been paying more attention than I thought.

"But as for Max, you need to put an end to this," she continues. "Whether you and Jaden survive doesn't rest on whether Max tells the owners or not. And that's if they *do* fire you guys. It's all up to you. Don't let that little punk kid push you around."

"Yeah, but—"

She shakes her head. "No buts. This could go on for a long time. The speculation among everyone else is going to do more harm than the actual secret. Get out in front of it and tell them yourself. Take away the power Max holds over you."

I wipe at my eyes, feeling kind of foolish for letting it get to me like this. "You're right. Tell everyone I want to have another meeting before they leave tonight."

"Good for you." She steps to the door.

"Hey Peggy?"

"Yeah?"

"Thanks."

She smiles. "No problem. Now show them the boss we all know."

Chapter Twelve:

JADEN

"Let's go, J-Man! Your girlfriend's waiting!" Max mutters over my shoulder as he passes by.

I give him a shove. He looks at me with warning in his eyes, so I dig my hands in my pockets to keep them still.

Peggy said that this meeting was important. Nobody really complained because we'll be getting paid extra for being here longer. I'm more worried about Robyn, though. Besides this morning, I haven't seen her at all today. She usually makes her rounds a few times a day. Especially on hot days like today when she passes out water. And she said she'd help clean too.

I settle onto a bench in the back of the break room as I wait for the rest of my coworkers to file in. Robyn still isn't out here and the office door is closed, like it's been all day. I don't like that. It's certainly not going to help her case with the rest of the workers.

It suddenly hits me: what if she's in there because of me? Not because of what Max made her promise the other day, but about what we said during our argument on the way back from the bonfire.

I hope I didn't make her that upset. I really wish I hadn't said that nobody liked her. That's just not true. No matter how mad or annoyed I was, I should've never made her feel so bad that she would lock herself in the office all day. I should've called her last night and apologized. Or anytime today. I've had so many chances.

There's a buzz throughout the room as everyone speculates what the meeting is about. I catch a few far-fetched ideas:

"Maybe she's quitting."

"Maybe we're getting a roller coaster!"

"Maybe sales are down and we're closing up shop."

The room silences as soon as the office door opens. Robyn steps out and looks around to make sure she has everyone's attention.

"Thanks for sticking around. I promise I won't keep you long," she starts. "Now, I have a lot to say and I don't want to be interrupted, so please, no questions until after I'm done, thanks."

It's like her own mini-press conference.

"In such a small town—and such a small workplace—rumors can take off quite rapidly, as I'm sure you all know. Whether it's a simple misunderstanding or something said with malice, fictitious stories have a way of spreading in places like Montana Beach or even right here at the Pier."

I can't believe she's talking about this. I want her to stop, put on the brakes. Not for me, but for her. She has a lot more at stake here. This was just a little summer job for me. I don't mind if I get fired. Well, I do, but it won't have as big of an effect on me.

"The only way to battle these rumors is to be open and honest about them," she continues. "For the last several weeks, I've been seeing an employee here at the Pier."

I lock eyes with Robyn as everyone murmurs around me,

guessing who she's been with. My name comes up a few times and I'm sure some of them notice the way Robyn and I are looking at each other, but at this moment I don't care. I only want to be sure Robyn's okay and she knows what she's doing.

"That's not right," Carl calls out from my right.

"Bet he had the easiest hours," Anthony adds, glancing in my direction.

Max puts his hand in the air and looks around the room. He raises his voice until everyone's quiet. "Can I just say that I think it's funny in the most ironic way that Robyn has always been quick to point out *our* faults, but she hasn't been upfront about her own all summer?"

The room erupts again, agreeing with Max, echoing what he said, and shouting further things at Robyn. She has one arm wrapped around her and is stroking her forehead with the other.

"Hey!" Peggy calls. "You're not supposed to talk until she's done!"

"Are you on her side now?" Max shouts back at her. "Who have *you* been sleeping with?"

The room's volume jumps up again, but I can't take my eyes off Robyn. I don't want her to break down in front of everybody. Max wouldn't let her forget it and that's exactly what she wants them to do—forget this issue altogether.

After another minute, I shoot up out of my seat and stand on the bench. Several people take notice, but it's not until I cry out, "Hey!" that everyone stops talking to give me their full attention.

"You're all being completely unfair to Robyn, you know that?" I say. "She's trying to do the right thing by being honest with you and you're so quick to tear her down. Yeah, she can come off as strict sometimes, but that's only because she wants this place—and the rest of you—to be the best that it can be." I look over at her. "That's what she's always looking for."

I take in the rest of the room. I know most of them have

figured it out or suspected—they certainly have now—but in following Robyn's lead, I need to be honest with them, too.

"I'm the one Robyn's been seeing all summer."

"No wonder you've been working so hard—"

"Max, would you *shut up* for once?" I cut him off. A few people smile. "Robyn wanted to keep it a secret because she didn't want the rest of you to think that she was showing favoritism to me."

"I think she was showing *plenty* of favoritism," Max says with a smirk. "She's never yelled at you."

"That's because I do my job, jackass," I shoot back. "She's always yelling at lazy people like you who can't even sweep the deck properly." I look around the room. "We're working at an amusement park that mostly caters to little kids. This is supposed to be fun! It's seasonal work and it's not that hard. Our job is to make someone smile every day, isn't that what Robyn was trying to tell us this morning?"

I see a few people nod in agreement. Max is still silent. Brooding. Well, pouting is more like it.

Robyn's watching me with a hint of a smile on her face, but I force myself to look away from her to continue. "Robyn wants to make sure that the Pier stays open for our customers—for all of us—and, sure, for herself too. She loves this job and she wants to keep it." I motion to Max. "But some people wanted to tell the owners about her relationship with me so that he could get what he wanted from her."

Bailey, Mackenzie, and a few others glare at him.

"What I'm sure we're all aware of is the fact that this place wouldn't be half as good if Robyn wasn't the one leading the rest of us," I say. "Sure, she's tough, but that just brings out the best in everyone."

Julie rolls her eyes. "Okay, I agree that you both should be able to do whatever you want outside of work. I also agree that

Robyn is great at her job, but I'm not convinced she's the only reason it's still open. There were other managers before her."

I nod. "You're right, she's not the only reason. We *all* are the reason. But we're the reason because *Robyn* pushes us to do our best. Before she came on board, the Pier was heading straight into the ground. Now, thanks to her and the motivation she gives us, it has a long future ahead of it. That is, if she doesn't get fired over something stupid."

"Favoritism isn't such a stupid reason," Max says. "You're just saying—"

"Dude, just stop," Michael says from by the door.

I look to Robyn to try to hide my smile, but it only grows more. "Listen," I say to the rest of the room, "I get it, if you don't like the idea that she's seeing an employee, that's fine. I'll quit. But don't jeopardize Robyn's job over this."

"We don't want you to go, man," Carl says.

The rest of the room echoes his thoughts. It makes me smile.

"But what's the plan going forward?" Bailey asks. "There's no way you *can't* favor him."

"We'll do our best," Robyn says. "Look, if I can be strict with you guys, I can be strict in my relationship, too. We'll check it at the door when we come to work. If any of you thinks I'm showing favoritism, come talk to me about it and we can work it out."

Everyone seems to nod in agreement.

"So what do you say?" I ask. "Can we keep it quiet from the owners? Just in case they ever decide to come down here?"

The room is painfully quiet for what feels like forever until Anthony says, "Don't worry about it. We've got your back." The rest of the room agrees.

"Thank you, everyone." Robyn smiles. She looks like she's about to cry. This time for a good reason.

Everyone starts to shuffle out except Max and Peggy. She's beside Robyn, asking if she's okay.

"Yeah," Robyn says. "I'll be fine. Thanks for today. You've been a big help. I really appreciate it."

"This is bullshit," Max says suddenly. "Why should you two get special treatment?"

Peggy nods to the door. "Grab your things, Max. I'll walk you out."

"No need." He snatches his bag from by his feet. "I quit."

"Wait, Max," I call to him. He stops in the doorway and looks at me. "I think you should find a new place to live, too. Maybe you can get your old bedroom back at your mom's?"

He flips me the bird and stalks off.

When the door slams shut, the three of us laugh.

"Well, I think that's solved a few problems," Peggy says. "You might want to make sure he doesn't vandalize your stuff, though," she tells me.

"Yeah, I should probably head over there now." I hop off the bench and step closer to Robyn.

Peggy takes note and says, "You two can close up, right? I'll see you tomorrow, Robyn. Have a nice night, Jaden." She grabs her purse from the office and then walks out.

"Well, that's—" I start, but Robyn's kiss cuts me off.

When she pulls away, she says, "I'm sorry if that was—I just thought—I mean, you said those things—I'm sorry for what I said last night."

I nod. "So am I. I know now that you were never embarrassed by me. I was overreacting. You were just scared about your job and everything. I see that now."

She looks down at our feet and tucks some of her hair behind her ear. "Yeah, basically."

I use my finger to tilt her chin up and kiss her again. "I've missed you."

She giggles. "It's only been one day."

I shake my head. "Doesn't matter. Still missed you."

"I missed you too."

"I've realized that I hate being apart from you," I say. "I love you, Robyn. And I know it's all so fast and it's okay if you don't feel—"

She kisses me again. "I love you, too."

I smile. "Really?"

"Yeah."

I wrap my arms around her and pick her up. She laughs until I set her back on her feet.

"Are we crazy?" I ask. "Two months ago we didn't even know each other."

She shrugs. "I've decided that it's better not to question these things."

We kiss once more and go into the office to finish closing out the Pier. After we're done, we head out to walk home.

"Guess I'm looking for another roommate," I say.

"Are you sure?" She takes my hand as we walk.

"Well, yeah, I'll have a hard time making the rent on my own. That's why I had Max move in to begin with."

Robyn scrunches her nose and shakes her head. "That house is too big for you."

I shrug. "Well, it's what I've got."

She throws her head back and rolls her eyes. "You are insanely bad at this. I'm saying you could stay with me."

I give her a look. "Are you sure? You don't think that's too fast?"

"This is *all* so fast. I'm not saying you should move in permanently, but you could stay the rest of the summer. Consider it a test run for the future. That'll help me decide if you drive me nuts. Besides, if we don't get to act like a couple here, we'll have to take full advantage at home."

Stopping on the sidewalk at the end of First Street, I lean down and kiss her. "I'd like that a lot."

"Good." The sun shines on her face.

"You know what's going to be one of my favorite parts of living with you?" I ask.

"What's that?"

"Seeing the light reflect in those beautiful sunset eyes every day."

§ § §

Pick up Summer Nights, Montana Beach, Book 3!
DavidNethBooks.com/SummerNights

Summer Job

Behind the Book

This was another book that only took me a week to write the first draft. Ever since I read Stephen King's *Joyland*, I knew I wanted to write a book that is set at an amusement park. Especially an old and forgotten one. I think it's so interesting to read about and see pictures of "forgotten" amusement parks. They were made with the expectation that there would be a lot of people, but when the business end of things gets too much, they shut down and nature starts to take it back. It's interesting.

Anyway, I had basically set the stage for Robyn and Jaden's story in *Summer Stay*, but I really got to dive into it here. It was even a little nostalgic to write in this setting because my first job was at an amusement park where we had morning meetings, was told to make people smile, and had to drink a lot of water throughout the day. I was definitely more like Max in those days because I hated that job, but it was my first job! I would've hated any job at that point in my life.

David Neth

This book didn't really dive into Montana Beach as the town that much, but I wanted to make it real by pointing out that this small town—like a lot of small towns—relies heavily on only a few successful business ventures, which might not be doing so hot. If those businesses go away, there's a lot of uncertainty for the future of the town. The stress of all that could weigh heavily on the person who has to make the decision to close up shop or not—which is exactly what Robyn goes through in Chapter 11.

Maybe in future books I'll make the town more successful. I haven't decided yet. I like that it's kind of frozen in time, which is why I set it up to be the antithesis of North Beach, which I envision as something like Virginia Beach or Myrtle Beach: tourist traps. Montana Beach is just a quiet little town that was settled by people who wanted to take a break from the world. At least, that's the tone I'm going for in these books. Feel free to email me or message me on social media to tell me otherwise.

As always, I hope you enjoyed this installment of the Montana Beach series. Maybe you read it by the pool, on a plane to tropical retreat, or even in the middle of winter. Either way, I hope it offered you some sort of escape from the real world. That's what people go to Montana Beach for!

DavidNethBooks.com/Newsletter

§ § §

On the surface Adrian has it all: he's the owner of the Nine—the only source of nightlife in Montana Beach—and he has his boyfriend Malcolm. The only problem is: Malcolm's married. Although he promises to leave his wife, Adrian still wonders if he'll always be "the other lover," and whether that's enough for him.

Tyler has watched his best friend pursue his relationship with a married man knowing that it won't end well. He knows that he could treat Adrian better, but he's never expressed his feelings to anyone, let alone Adrian.

After Adrian and Tyler share a special evening together, Tyler sees a future for them, but Adrian is still loyal to Malcolm.

§ § §

I'll be home for Christmas...

Tracy Slater may be a successful pop star, but fame and fortune isn't everything she thought it'd be. Under the thumb of a husband who is growing steadily more abusive, she's decided her marriage is over. She just needs to make it through one more trip home for the holidays with him before she's free.

If only in my dreams...

Stephen Austin worked hard to become the successful novelist he's always wanted to be. So why isn't he happy? And why does he feel so lonely? Then he runs into his old girlfriend, the one he thought he had lost forever.

Tormented by the mistakes of their past, Stephen sees his reunion with Tracy as a second chance. But does she feel the same way?

§ § §

Available in ebook, paperback, and audio!
DavidNethBooks.com/AChristmasReunion

A chance moment. A snow storm. And the gift of a new beginning.

Tristan is ready to party and ring in the New Year by kissing his soon-to-be girlfriend, Julie. The only bad note in his rocking night is the growing snow storm. Outside his apartment, he's almost hit by Grace, the most beautiful woman with haunting green eyes. She's on her own mission to get home to her grandfather.

In a selfless act reminiscent of the age of knights and chivalry, Tristan vows to get her home...never realizing they are both on a date with destiny and their lives will be forever changed by the SNOW AFTER CHRISTMAS...

§ § §

Available in ebook, paperback, and audio!
DavidNethBooks.com/SnowAfterChristmas

More by the Author

To find the rest of the author's books visit
DavidNethBooks.com/Books

§ § §

Subscribe to his newsletter to be the first to know of new releases and special deals!
DavidNethBooks.com/Newsletter

§ § §

If you enjoyed the book, please consider leaving a review on Goodreads or the retailer you bought it from. Reviews help potential readers determine whether they'll enjoy a book, so any comments on what you thought of the story would be very helpful!

About the Author

David Neth is the author of the Fuse series, the Montana Beach series, the Small Town Christmas series, the Under the Moon series, and other stories. He lives in Batavia, NY, where he dreams of a successful publishing career and opening his own bookstore.

§ § §

Follow the author at

www.DavidNethBooks.com
www.facebook.com/DavidNethBooks
www.twitter.com/DavidNethBooks
www.instagram.com/dneth13

Made in the USA
Coppell, TX
19 October 2021